A
Charming Magic

Tonya Kappes

Dedication

This book is dedicated to all my readers who absolutely love visiting Whispering Falls as much as I do! You all rock!

Chapter One

"Today is the day!" Chandra Shango shouted over to me when I walked out of the door of my homeopathic cure shop, A Charming Cure. The morning sun sprayed down exposing the dew drops on the Drowsy Daisies and Moonflower petals that had already opened up to let the bit of vitamin D put more pep in the more-than-colorful flowers.

"It is." I stopped and smiled watching Chandra go down the row of flower boxes underneath the windows of her shop, A Cleansing Spirit Spa, wiping off the dots of water on each and every single petal, adjusting her orange turban with each step she took.

My charm bracelet jingled when I flung my bag over my shoulder and gripped a good luck mojo bag in my hand. The welcome sounds from my bracelet gave me peace to know that I was safe and sound, not to mention that I was well looked after by Mr. Prince Charming, my fairy-god cat.

Meow. Purr. Mr. Prince Charming stood next to me slowly waging his long white tail in the air.

I looked up and down Main Street in Whispering Falls, Kentucky. The carriage lights lined the magical street showcasing all the beautiful ornamental gates leading up to the coziest shops this side of the Mississippi, adding to how enchanting the town was.

"Let's go," I said.

Meow, meow. Mr. Prince Charming darted out from under my feet and through the wisteria vine covering the path in front of my shop. The purple flowers overflowed and jumped out of the path of feet and other invading critters.

"Thank you." I watched my footing making sure I didn't step on any of the vine.

"Well, well. Aren't you just the best Village President?" Petunia Shrubwood had bent down to pet Mr. Prince Charming while he did his signature figure eights around her ankles. He loved a good scratch and ankles were his choice of pleasure. "I see you have a mojo bag," she pointed.

"I have yet to meet our new neighbor." I glanced over my right shoulder where Magical Moments, the new shop, was located. It wasn't just any new shop. It was a flower shop. "I'm going to take over a few good luck charms and introduce myself."

Petunia grabbed a stick off the ground before she stood up and tugged the crease out of her A-framed black skirt with bright yellow polka dots all over it.

"No one has seen the new owner since *they* put these things up so fast." She put the stick in her messy up-do, referring to how fast shops seemed to appear out of nowhere.

Chirp, chirp. A couple of birds flew out the back of her hair allowing her to push the stick in even further.

"The Marys are fast," I referred to the Order of Elders of the Spiritualist community, Mary Lynn, Mary Ellen, and Mary Sue. Affectionately known as the Marys.

The Order of Elders was made up of past Village Presidents from other spiritual communities. They were in charge of all of the villages, including new shops. As the Whispering Falls Village President, my only duties consisted of making sure the rules were followed and peace was kept within the community. So far, so good. At least for the past six months.

"I guess it went up overnight." I looked over at the charming new shop. The front gate looked like long-stemmed flowers with the blossoms on the top. Perfect for a florist.

"Overnight?" Petunia laughed. "I had late tea with Gerald at The Gathering Grove last night." She blushed. "I guess you could say early morning tea." She looked away obviously remembering her time with her long-time boyfriend, Gerald Regiula, who owned The Gathering Grove Tea Shoppe, which was almost directly across the street from the Magical Moments. "It was not there when I came home."

I didn't ask what time she went home from her late night tryst and really didn't care since my love life was dead.

"Yes." I inhaled trying to push the thought of Oscar Park out of my head. I had a lot of work to do today and thinking about Oscar was not on that list. If it was, nothing would get done. "The Marys work fast." I dangled the bag in the air. "I guess I will see you later."

"I'm going with you." She pulled a little bag out from underneath her cloak. "I have some good luck bugs to give her."

"Bugs?" I asked. Bugs couldn't be good for a florist, could they?

"Yes. Bugs," was all she said. She should know since she was the owner of Glorybee Pet Shop. "These bugs keep the bad bugs out." She beamed with pride. "At least that was what they said." Her cheeks balled.

We walked the little distance to the front of the flower shop. We both took a deep breath. The fresh cut smell circled our heads and flew up into the air. I was sure I'd be able to get a whiff of the wonderful scents from my house which was situated on the hill right behind the florist.

Petunia Shrubwood's spiritual gift was the ability to talk to animals while mine was the ability to create cures for all sorts of things.

I couldn't wait to see what the new tenant's spiritual gift was. That was what made Whispering Falls so special. Every single shop owner had an unusual spiritual gift.

Petunia's boyfriend, Gerald, was a tea leaf reader, hence the reason he owned The Gathering Grove. Chandra was a palm reader. Her customers loved her. They were regulars, coming back for more of Chandra's advice even though they had no idea she was a palm reader. All they knew was that Chandra was magical.

"Yes, it should be interesting to see what talent this one has." Petunia's eyes narrowed as she bobbled her head back and forth trying to get a look inside the gate.

"Petunia! You whoooo!" Patience Karima could be heard but not seen. The only thing we saw was the berserk giant ostrich Patience had acquired as a pet, only I think it acquired her.

The large feathery bird flew right past us with Patience dangling in the air behind the squawking creature. Eyes shut, mouth open, and hands tightly holding on to the leash.

"Help!" Patience's voice trailed off as the bird darted out of sight.

"I guess this will have to wait." Petunia opened her cloak and put the bag of bugs back underneath it. She waved. "I've already told her how to be an ostrich owner." Petunia shook her head before heading after Patience.

The clouds parted allowing the sunlight to beam down on Whispering Falls in full force. The carriage lights clicked off. It was almost time for the shops to open.

I placed my hand on the gate of Magical Moments to open it. It was like one of those mood rings I had as a child. The iron stems turned green and the blossoms turned into

every color of the rainbow, creating a little garden right
there on the gate.

   "Well, isn't that cute." My spirit filled with joy.
Instantly I knew I was going to love the shop owner; they
were going to fit in perfectly.

Chapter Two

"Rules, rules, rules!" A pair of thin hands shot up in the air behind a bundle of the most beautiful bouquet of long-stemmed white roses, which everyone who knew anything about magic—or roses for that matter—knew was a sign of a new beginning. The snip of scissors clicked faster and faster. Several green stems flew up in the air. I ducked when one hurtled my way. "Who can live with all these rules?"

"You need a fresh start and I stuck my neck out for you." The small sweet voice came from the area where the stems flew up. A flash of light sailed into the air illuminating the floating woman underneath it. Her silver tight curls and fox stole resting around her neck gave me a clue who she was before she had to turn around. "Whispering Falls is a forgiving community. You will follow the rules." She crossed her arms just like her legs were.

Ahem. I cleared my throat. Though I was the Village President, I didn't have the right to be eavesdropping. "Welcome to Whispering Falls." Nervously I tucked a strand of my black hair behind my ear and tugged on my long black dress. It drove me crazy when the side seams began to shift to the front of my body. "I brought you a congratulations mojo bag to welcome you to the community."

Mary Lynn, one of the Order of Elders and the hovering spiritualist, turned her head. She smiled and uncurled her arms and legs, letting the light bring her feet to the ground. Only I couldn't see her once she was firmly on the ground since she was only four feet tall, but I could hear the click of her pointy black shoes as she got closer to the front of the store.

There was a small creek running through the store. On each side were tiered black display tables with lines of black vases filled with all sorts of bright and colorful flowers. Darla, my mom, would have loved this shop. The owner had to be happy all the time. There was no way anyone could ever have a bad day around such amazing colors and smells. My eyes filled with amazement at all the wonderful items I could possibly use in new cures. I would definitely have to make arrangements with the owner to get fresh herbs and ingredients.

"June!" Mary Lynn turned the corner next to a small claw-foot table where there was a beautiful flower arrangement strategically placed in the center. The large glass purple vase was bigger than Mary Lynn, not to mention the bouquet reached the ceiling of the flower shop. "I'm so glad you are here."

"*Ecstatic*," a sarcastic voice was barely heard over the sound of the snipping scissors.

"It's my pleasure." I tilted my head to the side to see if I could get a look at the new shop owner. I held the mojo bag up while Mary Lynn wrapped her arms around my waist to give me a big hug.

She pulled back and teetered on the edge of the small creek. I pulled her closer to me and off the edge of the water.

"How are you, dear?" There was a concerned tone to her voice. The corners of her eyes dipped down on the sides.

"I'm doing okay." I smiled trying not to cry. Mary Lynn was one of the Elders who Oscar had denounced his spiritual gift to. She was there to help pick me up when I found out. "I have come to realize Oscar will never be able to accept me as his girlfriend or remember the fact that he was truly in love with me and this life."

"So this Oscar doesn't have a girlfriend?" The snipping stopped. The sound of heels clicked closer and out from behind the flower arrangements on the other side of the creek.

"I…I," I swallowed hard when the dark-haired beauty walked up. Her olive skin went perfect with her deep blue eyes and high cheek bones, making me a little envious. "I'm June Heal, the owner of A Charming Cure." I pointed out the door. "Just next door a little bit."

"A little bit?" Her right brow rose as though she didn't believe me.

"Um..." I held out the mojo bag. "This is for you. It's a mojo bag filled with good luck charms and smells."

"As you can see," the scissors were still in her hand and she turned to snip a flower in the flower bed that lined the creek. "I have plenty of smells to keep me happy and filled with luck. Who doesn't love a flower shop? A magical flower shop?"

"June, this is my granddaughter, Arabella Paxton." Mary Lynn hopped her small body over the creek, barely clearing it. She put her hands on Arabella's arms. "She's amazing with flowers."

"I'm a floral designer." Arabella's ice blue eyes narrowed, a thin grin crossed her lips causing her already high cheekbones to be even more defined. She flung the scissors around in the air. "What was this about a girlfriend-free Oscar? I wondered what type of men were in this community. And I need a man."

"I'm also the Village President." I took a deep breath. Suddenly I had all sorts of confidence. There was no way this woman was going to get her flower shears on my man. Okay...technically Oscar wasn't my man, but he was and will be...one day. "Do you have a copy of the rules of the community?"

I recalled her fussing about rules when I had walked in.

"June," Arabella threw her head back, her long straight hair cascading down her back. Her mouth opened wide and a fit of laughter came out. "Do you honestly think I didn't know you were standing here when my sweet dear grandmother was scolding me about the rules?" She smiled. "You underestimate me."

Not only was she beautiful and smart, but also she was a smart aleck.

"Oh Arabella." I was going to give it right back to her. "I don't underestimate anyone moving into *my* community. I do, however, expect you to follow the rules."

My intuition dug into my gut. Where did she come from? Why did she move here?

"You should follow your own rule of not trying to read other spiritualists," she reminded me of Rule Number One. "Because I don't recall me giving you permission."

Not only did I have the spiritual gift of knowing what potions to make for any type of ailment, but I had a keen since of intuition. But how did she know that?

"I'm sorry if you felt like I was reading you, but I was not." My shoulders rolled back so I could gain more confidence. I held out the bag, across the creek. "I did overhear you and Mary Lynn discussing the rules when I walked in. It's just a gentle reminder. That's all."

Her long lean fingers reached out and grabbed the bag. The bag fell and splashed into the water.

"Oops." She put her hand over her mouth. "I guess I didn't have a good grip."

"Arabella." Mary Lynn gasped and reached into the water to get the bag. She held it up. The wet herbs inside the bag had stained the cheese cloth bag and drips of black splattered on the floor.

"Oh Grandmother!" Arabella grabbed the bag and disappeared to where she had come from. The clunk of the bag echoed when she tossed it in the trash.

"I'm so sorry," Mary Lynn profusely apologized. "She's having a hard time moving here."

"And why exactly is she here?" I asked.

"Grandmother?" Arabella's voice had changed into a sweet voice. If I hadn't had my interaction with her, I would have been fooled by the innocent tone. "If we are ever going to get the shop opened in five minutes, I'm going to need your help."

"I'm sorry." Mary Lynn wrung her hands as she shook her head. Quickly she turned and rushed back to her granddaughter.

Arabella's head popped up above the back display shelf. Her eyes caught mine. She glared a moment too long before the evil grin crossed her face.

"Be sure to tell Oscar to stop in for a free flower." She held up a red rose and twirled it in her fingers before she lifted it to her nose. "Oh, and I'd be more than happy to give you my leftovers for your little cure shop especially if I'm going to take your leftover." She winked and disappeared back behind the display table, not wasting a moment to start clipping away.

Chapter Three

"My leftover?" I stomped my way out of the shop and through the gate, nearly knocking right into Petunia Shrubwood. "Oscar Park is not a leftover! Over my dead body!"

"Whoa!" Petunia stepped out of the way, the bag of bugs dangling from her wrist. Patience and her ostrich did another fly by. "First, Patience. Now you?" She shook her head.

I glared at her and stepped off the sidewalk into the street. I kept walking. My eyes set on my shop.

"Her leftovers over my dead body!" I screamed over my shoulder. "*Arabella Paxton.*" I curled my nose when I said her name. My hands fisted at my side. "I will just keep getting my herbs from KJ."

Potions, bad potions, and things I could do to Arabella whirled around in my head. The wind whipped up along with my thoughts. The leaves blew up and around my body before twirling up to the sky like a tornado. KJ was the Native American I got my ingredients and herbs from when I ran out.

Beep, beep. The honking horn nearly made me jump out of my skin.

"You better get out of the way." The window rolled down and Oscar Park popped his head out. He held up a cup of coffee. "You look like you need this!"

Relief settled in my soul and the tension left my shoulders. I didn't need coffee. I needed him. Just looking at his bright white smile that led up to his twinkling blue eyes, made anything wrong melt away and fade off.

"Park." My charm bracelet jingled as I pointed to a parking spot right in front of the shop. I had ten minutes before I had to open A Charming Cure, and I couldn't think of any better way to spend it. I walked toward him.

"Yea, you definitely looked frazzled." Oscar looked at his watch before he got out of the car. "And it's only nine a.m." He laughed and held out the cup of coffee from Wicked Good.

"Yum." I could smell the delicious fresh java he had bought from the shop a couple of doors down.

Wicked Good was owned and operated by one of my dear friends, Raven Mortimer, who happened to name a homemade pastry after me, June's Gems.

"Don't think I forgot this too." Oscar winked and retrieved a green and pink Wicked Good bag from the front seat of his car.

"You are a life saver." My mouth watered at the chocolaty treat inside the bag.

"Oh dear." The voice came from the sidewalk causing Oscar and I to look over. "I didn't realize this was so heavy."

Arabella stood on the sidewalk next to the most amazing flower sculpture I had ever laid eyes on. Her leg was cocked to the side and her hands were planted on her slim hips. Her long black hair flowed over her shoulder as she tilted her head as if she was confused.

Her eyes slid over to us, catching Oscar's attention. When they made eye contact she smiled. Her eyes narrowed and she pointed to him.

"You," her voice purred. "You look like a big strong man that can help me."

"Of course." Oscar wasted no time handing me his cup of coffee.

"No!" I protested while trying to juggle the cups and the bag. Oscar stopped. There was a puzzled look on his handsome tan face. "I mean, no to holding all of this."

"I'll be right back," he said.

He might be right back, but his heart might not be. I lowered my eyes and glared at her. She didn't take her eyes off of him. As a matter of fact, I swore I saw her look him up and down with a wanting look only another woman would know.

"That's amazing." Oscar pointed to the design.

Arabella had taken a body form and used hot pink flowers to make a flowing skirt. There were fabric butterflies strategically placed all over the bodice of the silhouette and in the flowery hair Arabella had created. It was beautiful, but I would have never told her that.

"Thank you." Arabella dragged her long fingernail down Oscar's muscular arm, sending my gut into a fit of rage. I knew exactly what she was trying to do. "You must be Oscar."

Oscar blushed. I rolled my eyes.

"I'm Arabella Paxton." She spoke loud enough for me to hear her and held her hand out for him to take.

Oscar did something I had never seen before. He took the tip of her fingers, like you would see in an old movie, bringing the back of her hand to his lips and he kissed it.

"Nice to meet you." His country accent sent her into a fit of laughter.

"Aren't you a true southern gentleman?" Arabella pulled her hand away and held it to her chest.

Ahem. I cleared my throat raising both my brows.

"I guess your girlfriend is summoning you so if you could help me get this up the steps and position it for the world to see and want to come in to check out our grand opening." She turned and sashayed her way to the spot where she wanted Oscar to put the flowery arrangement.

My mouth dropped. *Disgusting,* I thought as I watched her butt swing side to side and Oscar's eyes follow.

"June?" Oscar laughed. "June isn't my girlfriend. She's my best friend."

"Oscar does not live in Whispering Falls!" I hollered over to Arabella so she would know he wasn't a spiritualist. Technically he was, but now he wasn't. No. Thanks. To. Me.

Mewl. Mr. Prince Charming shared my disgust. He stretched his paws out in front of him and shook each back leg before he darted up the steps of A Charming Cure.

"I guess you are right." I looked over at Mr. Prince Charming. It was time to open, but if I knew Mr. Prince Charming like I knew I did, he too wasn't happy with Arabella's sudden need when we both knew she was capable of handling a little mannequin of flowers on her own.

"So where do you live?" Arabella's soft sweet voice echoed down the street right into my ears. I cringed hearing her.

"Locust Grove." Oscar was being charmed by her sudden interest. "It's just right outside of Whispering Falls. Where are you from?"

As I walked up the steps to the shop, I glanced down sliding my eyes toward Oscar, trying to be sly like a fox, only Arabella was waiting for me to look at them.

"I'm from another spirit..." she paused and bit her lip. "I'm from up north."

Oscar lifted the mannequin with one hand. Arabella stood behind him placing her hands on each of his shoulders as if she was steering him up the steps where she wanted the large floral arrangement to go.

"You sure have some great muscles."

I nearly gagged hearing her flirt with him. Surely he wouldn't fall for it and would see right through her. I put the coffees on the ground and jiggled the door handle a couple of times to prolong my painful torture of listening to Arabella try to woo Oscar. *If she only knew,* I laughed out loud. There was no way he was going to fall for someone like her.

"I have to stay in shape being the sheriff of Locust Grove, ya know." Oscar sounded smitten, but there was no way. No way. There had better not be a way. My eyes narrowed.

God golly. Was he really falling for that crap Arabella was feeding him?

"Sheriff?" Arabella squealed. "I love a man in uniform."

Oscar set the flowered mannequin exactly where she was pointing. He glanced over at me. I jerked my head to the side so he would know I was telling him to come on.

"Speaking of work." He rubbed his hands together before he pointed over to A Charming Cure. "Nice to meet you…" He searched for her name, apparently already forgetting it.

"Arabella Paxton." She put her hand out for him to take. Again, he did that thing where he kissed her freaking hand before he dropped it and skipped down the steps. She hollered after him, "Oscar, you are more than welcome to stop in anytime."

"Are you kidding me?" I asked under my breath when he trotted through the gate and up the steps of A Charming Cure.

"What?" He picked up the coffees as I unlocked the door. "It took you a while to open the door," he observed. "Or were you being nosy?"

"Me? Nosy?" I scoffed and felt for the light switch just inside the door.

Mr. Prince Charming darted into the shop once the lights illuminated the space and jumped on the counter, his favorite spot.

"Yes, nosy you," Oscar joked and made his way back to set the coffees next to Mr. Prince Charming. "Interesting." Oscar picked something up off the counter next to Mr. Prince Charming's paws. "I see your crazy cat is still up to his old ways." He held something in the air for me to see. "One of these days someone is going to catch him for stealing and he will be out of lives then."

Oscar's voice was white noise. My eyes zeroed in on the shiny thing dangling between his finger and thumb.

Normally I would rush around the shop and straighten the red tablecloths on all the round display tables, or refill and reposition some of the potion bottles that held my homeopathic cures, but not today.

I ran back to see exactly what Oscar had picked up. Yes. Mr. Prince Charming was good at giving me a charm. But only when there was going to be some sort of danger.

I took a deep breath and held out my hand for Oscar to drop the shiny item into it as I tried to tap into my intuition. Nothing. Nothing alarmed me that there was something bad going to happen.

Rowl! Mr. Prince Charming hopped off the counter and darted underneath one of the round display tables, nearly toppling a few of the bottles over.

It was another charm. Another charm to add to my ever-growing charm bracelet.

A dove sitting on a round thin piece of gold. The round piece looked an awful lot like a wedding ring. *Wedding ring?* I glanced up at Oscar. I smiled. *A wedding ring.*

Was it a sign? Did this have anything to do with my past history with Oscar? The romantic history he didn't remember?

It all happened on my tenth birthday. Darla, my mom—a single mom—spent all her time running her homeopathic cure shop, A Dose of Darla, out of a booth at the Locust Grove Flea Market and she didn't have a ton of money to spend on my birthdays. Cake, card, and a candle from the flea market was as good as I was going to get. After all, it was my tenth birthday, not some big milestone like sixteen. And the cake…it was a "manager's special" cake that read *Happy Retirement Stu*. Darla didn't bother scraping it off or pretending it wasn't a manager's special. Don't get me wrong. It was a treat. Sugar snacks of any kind weren't allowed in the Heal household except on special occasions.

It was that same day that Darla was at work and I was at home hanging out with Oscar—yes, he lived across the street. Even then I was in love with him. Like any stupid boy, he didn't notice. Still, that day, was a day I will never forget and probably the best birthday I had ever had.

The pristine white cat jumped up on the porch wearing a worn-out collar with a turtle charm dangling off it. He had to belong to someone. A stray cat would have never been that clean, especially a white one. It looked like he was from a fairy tale, so I named him Mr. Prince Charming.

Oscar and I had spent countless hours trying to find Mr. Prince Charming's owner, but no one claimed him.

To beat the band, no one but Oscar knew that I had prayed so hard for a charm bracelet from Darla. There was a girl at school who had one. Every time I heard the jingle of her charms when she raised her hand and saw the beautiful silver slither down her small wrist, I grew green with envy. After school I would check my face in the mirror to make sure I wasn't green. I was so envious.

Oscar had even given me his mom's old bracelet for a birthday gift. It was the only thing he had left of her. Oscar's parents had died in a car wreck, leaving him orphaned like me.

Technically I wasn't orphaned because I had my mom, but she worked so much, it was like I was orphaned.

Anyway, since no one had claimed Mr. Prince Charming, I knew he was mine and so was that turtle charm. Oscar fastened the charm on his mom's bracelet with a bread tie and put it on my wrist. It was the best birthday ever, until every year after Mr. Prince Charming always brought me a charm to add to my bracelet. It was like he was magical.

It wasn't until I grew up and moved to Whispering Falls did I realize Mr. Prince Charming was in fact magical. Sort of. He was sent by the Whispering Falls Village Council to keep an eye on me. After all, I was a spiritualist and didn't know it. So the charms he gave me were protective charms.

Now when he gives me a protective charm, it's a good indication that something was going to go haywire. This was no ordinary charm. It was a wedding ring with a dove.

"June? Earth to June?" Oscar waved half of a June's Gem underneath my nose. I blinked, bringing myself back to the present where I now lived in Whispering Falls after finding out I was from a spiritualist family with an uncanny talent of being able to concoct crazy ingredients to heal people, not to mention my talent of an amazing intuition.

Oscar too moved to Whispering Falls the same time I did after taking the open sheriff's position, but denounced his wizardry talents when I got myself into a little hot water and the only way he could help me was to denounce his gift, leaving him with no memory what-so-ever of spiritual nature or more importantly, when he told me he loved me.

"I...," I stuttered and held the charm closer to my eyes. "I don't think this is like any of the other charms he has given me."

Slowly my eyes moved to the bottom of the table where Mr. Prince Charming's tail swept the floor in a back-and-forth motion. It was true. Mr. Prince Charming and Oscar had never been the best of friends. Even after eighteen years of being around each other.

My breath quickened. My eyes widened.

"Are you okay?" Oscar asked taking another bite out of the chocolaty treat. "All of the sudden you got pale." He stuffed the rest in his mouth. "You aren't going to faint, are you?" he asked with a mouthful.

"No." I smiled. Images of me in a wedding gown made me feel all warm and fuzzy inside. "Far from it."

Meow. Mr. Prince Charming peeked his head out from underneath the tablecloth.

Yes. A wedding ring. No wonder Mr. Prince Charming was mad. Oscar and I were going to finally be getting together. Especially now after Oscar finally accepted he was a spiritualist.

Eloise Sandlewood, Oscar's aunt and a local in Whispering Falls, and I told Oscar about his memory loss. We left out the part about our romance because I wanted him to fall back in love with me, not feel he was obligated. He was upset at first, but he has grown to accept it and that I too was a spiritualist. Luckily it didn't hurt our friendship.

Like I said, Mr. Prince Charming was a little jealous of my relationship with Oscar, which led me to believe the charm was a protection charm for marriage. After all, Mr. Prince Charming was my fairy-god cat and he was not allowed to discriminate on who or what he protected me from, even if his judgment was off, way off, on this one.

Chapter Four

Oscar flipped the open sign around when he left. Happily I took another sip of my coffee and walked behind the small partition on the other side of the counter where I flipped on my cauldron.

A wedding. I sighed. I looked up at the framed picture that hung on the wall of me, Darla and my dad and wished they were here to share in my good fortune. I rubbed the little dove charm while images of my dad walking me down the aisle played over and over in my mind.

They would have been so proud.

Bubble, bubble. The rapidly-boiling green frothy mix bubbled to the top of the new cauldron I had picked up from Wands, Potions, and Beyond while visiting my great-aunt Helena who was the dean at Hidden Halls, A Spiritualist University. My father's aunt. At least I had one relative still living.

In fact, I was still getting used to my new cauldron. It was like everything else. New and improved.

My last cauldron—my first cauldron—had a bad potion that shattered the darn thing into a million little pieces, leaving me without my magical pot to keep working on my love…um …memory potion for Oscar.

I reached over and rubbed my finger on the dove charm, making a metal note to take it to Bella's Baubles so Isabella Van Lou, Bella for short, could put the charm on my bracelet. Even more so, I couldn't wait to see her face, though I was sure that was where Mr. Prince Charming got the charm in the first place.

Sigh. With the new turn of events, it wasn't that I needed Oscar to remember, but it would be awful handy. I continued to stir the potion that I had started; a potion I was relying on to give him his memory back.

The thought of his dark hair and hot, hunky, well-built chest under Oscar's cop shirt were enough to get my inner cauldron boiling. Lazily I stirred the bubbling substance eagerly awaiting KJ to bring my beehive husk, which happened to be the one ingredient I didn't have on hand. The last ingredient I needed to finish my little concoction.

KJ blew in with the wind and out with the breeze, bringing me all the things I had ordered. Only this time he was about two weeks late. Which was not common. Once I put in an order, he was usually at A Charming Cure within a couple of days.

If I had to pick one thing about being a homeopathic spiritualist that kind of stunk, I couldn't just drive to the Piggly Wiggly in Locust Grove, Kentucky, I had to put out a call into the night wind. Yes. I had to stand out in the night air, lick my pointer finger and try to determine which way the wind was blowing. Once I figured that out, I had to shout out into the wind the things I needed. Things like beehive husk, bear claw, charred skeever hide, Dwarven oil, Glow Dust, you know…the basics.

Can you imagine me standing out in the midnight air in my bat pajamas with my chin-length bob pulled back into the smallest ponytail you had ever seen and my finger twitching around in the air? I was sure I looked like a fool licking my finger at least twenty times and putting it in the air. I definitely wasn't good at finding the wind, but somehow KJ always got my order.

The door of the shop flew open bringing in a couple of leaves rustling and dancing around before settling on the wood floor. The bell that hung over the door dinged back and forth several times before coming to a rest.

Meow, meow. Mr. Prince Charming ran out from underneath the table, followed by some heavy footsteps. He jumped up on the countertop and took his rightful spot.

"I see you are working hard back there." The strapping young Native American stood in the doorway of the shop with a bundle of sage, grass root, and beehive husks neatly tied up in the crook of his arm.

"KJ!" I took the ladle out of the cauldron and laid it down. I hurried around the counter to meet him.

I put my arms around KJ, practically crushing the bundle. The crackling dried leaves crumbled between us as I pulled him closer when my eyes caught sight of Oscar standing next to his car with Arabella leaning up against his door in a very provocative pose.

What the heck? He left a while ago.

My eyes narrowed as I watched Arabella hand Oscar a piece of paper. My stomach knotted when Oscar looked at the paper and a big smile crossed his face. Arabella ran her whole hand down his arm before she said goodbye and jogged off toward her store. Her hair swung back and forth. Oscar watched her the whole way.

KJ tried to pull away, but I grabbed him tighter. He patted me on the back. I could tell he thought I was crazy, but what homeopathic spiritualist wasn't? Especially one that was getting railroaded by another spiritualist.

"Good to see you too, June." KJ placed his hands on my shoulders and pushed off of me. He closed the door behind him and held the bundle out for me to take. "Beehive husk is hard to get this time of year. If you would have asked for Luna Moth Wings," he snapped his fingers, "I could have gotten it like that."

KJ continued to tell me the story of how he had to put several calls into the wind in order to get the beehive husk. And I only wished I had heard him, but I wasn't paying a bit of attention to the feisty young man with long black hair and deep brown eyes. If only Arabella were as nice as KJ, I would have gotten some items from her. There was no way

I was going to buy from her when she was bound and determined to get her thorns into my Oscar.

The beehive husk was a must.

I took a deep sigh and held the bundle close to my heart thinking about the charm and Oscar.

"June?" KJ waved his hand in front of me. "Did you hear what I just said?"

"Umm…" I shook my head. My short black bob swung side to side. "Yes."

"Yes, you do? Or yes, you don't?" KJ stared at me. He must have read my blank look. "The Luna Moth Wing?"

"Oh." I looked over my shoulder at the row of ingredients on the shelf behind the counter to see if my supply was low.

"It's the harvest time and I'm picking some up. If you need some, tell me now. That way you won't look so silly standing in the dark with your pajamas on trying to figure out how to get in touch with me. It's a very busy time of the year so I might be a few days late." An ornery smile crossed his tan face, exposing the most perfect set of white teeth I'd ever seen.

"A few days?" I asked in a joking way.

"Yea, yea. I'm sure you are mad that I'm a couple weeks late." He picked up a couple of different potion bottles sitting on one of the display tables in the middle of the room. He glanced up. There was a twinkle in his dark eyes. "By the way, are those bats glow-in-the-dark?"

"If you must know." I whacked him with the bundle before I put it on the counter. "They are! I love my bat pjs. And no."

"No what?" he asked. His brows narrowed and a puzzled look settled on his face, defining his strong jaw bone.

"No Luna Moth Wing." Even though I had a pinch left, I didn't see why I would need the unusual ingredient. After all, Luna Moth Wing was used in some sort of baby-making potions and there would be none of that around here at this time. Those types of potions were never on my mind so I really didn't know much about them. It was always good to have some on hand and the small amount I did have was going to be plenty.

KJ and I both turned to look as the bell dinged over the shop door.

"Good morning!" Ophelia Biblio traipsed in, looking so fashionable in her pointy bootie boots, skinny jeans, and purple flowy blouse. Her curly honey hair neatly spilled over her shoulders and cascaded down the front of her five-foot-five frame. In a high-pitched voice she said, "Have you been to the new florist yet? Divine! Absolutely divine." She brushed her hands in the air. "And that Arabella is so charming."

"*So charming*," a hint of sarcasm dripped out of my mouth. KJ and Ophelia looked at each other. "KJ, Ophelia Biblio." There was an introduction to be made. KJ was a young man, Ophelia was a young woman. Both hot. Both sweet. Only Ophelia was taken. Smitten in fact with Whispering Falls' newest police chief Colton Lance.

Who wouldn't fall for Colton's big, brown, puppy-dog eyes and messy blond hair that any woman would want to run their hands through?

I probably should have helped KJ pop his chin back in place, but I figured I'd let him drool a little bit longer. Ophelia was definitely a beauty. If I was a guy, I'd probably fall for her too.

"Nice to meet you." Ophelia dripped with sexy. She held her hand out for KJ to take. He did the good gentleman thing and kissed the top of it, just like Oscar had done to Arabella, only Oscar wasn't falling for Arabella's beauty like KJ was falling all over Ophelia.

"How is Colton?" I decided to let KJ's heart off the hook. I think his heart stopped. All the blood looked like it had drained from his face. I touched his arm. "Colton is the new sheriff in town and he's Ophelia's boyfriend."

"Oh." KJ's brows lifted. "It was nice to meet you." He nodded toward Ophelia, and then turned to me. I was so glad to see the nice olive complexion had returned to his cheeks. "If you need anything, June, I'll be looking for the glowing bats." He winked before a gush of wind blew the door wide open, rushing in to sweep him away.

"That's what I call service." Ophelia shut the door and dusted her hands off. "Now what do you need that for?" She pointed to the bundle KJ had brought.

"You never know when there is going to be a smudging ceremony." I went about my business straightening the bottles on the shelf and using the feather duster to dust around them. Ophelia was prying. Trying to figure out what I had up my sleeve with the beehive husk, but I wasn't going to tell her I was secretly making a potion to slip to Oscar to help with his memory loss. The issues between me and Oscar were just that. Between me and Oscar.

I picked up a jar that I figured KJ had left me. Inwardly I groaned at the sight of the jar of spiders. I didn't order spiders but there was a note attached. I shrugged it off and assumed it was a thank you note and placed the jar on the shelf with the other ingredients.

I turned back toward Ophelia. "How is Ever After?"

Ever After Book Store was a welcomed addition to Whispering Falls a few months ago. Everyone loved a good book, including me.

"Everything is well." She picked up the long thin green and blue glass bottle, Black of Night Potion. The cork popped when she took the lid off and sniffed the contents. "Oh, I think I need this."

It was unusual for a spiritualist to need a potion, or at least I thought it was.

"Really?" I questioned her. She was probably returning the favor of buying something from the shop since I was spending almost every single extra dime I had purchasing books from her store. I could never resist a good *Potion Making for Dummies* book and Ever After had the best selection. "You don't need a sleeping potion."

"I don't. But Colton does," she quipped. "I'm not getting any sleep because he is snoring. This might do the trick." She pointed to the label. "It says here that it helps with snoring."

"It does." In fact, I sold a lot of Black of Night to many wives. It seemed that every man had started to snore, keeping the wife up all night. Every household knows that when the woman didn't get the sleep she required, you'd better watch out. I walked behind the counter and with my back to Ophelia, I dusted the ingredients shelf.

"Wonderful." She saddled up to the counter where Mr. Prince Charming was and raked her long nails along his back. His body curved like a wave. "A word to the wise," Ophelia drew in a breath. The shop lights flickered. An uneasy feeling gathered at the top of my stomach and at the base of my throat. "You should have taken some Luna Moth Wing."

"How did you know he asked me about that?" I turned around with the duster waving in the air. Feathers flew all over the place. "Ophelia?"

I did a three-hundred-and-sixty degree turn to find her. Like KJ, she was gone. I walked over to the door and peered out the window to see if I could find her.

"She's sure making her rounds." I tilted my head to the side to see better around the curtains.

Arabella was standing in the middle of the street talking to Gerald Regiula. Talking was an understatement. They were in a deep conversation, Gerald leaning a bit too much into Arabella's hair if anyone was to ask me. But no one was, so I stepped back, ran my hands down the front of my shirt before I bent down to pat Mr. Prince Charming who had made his way over to my ankles.

Mewl. Mr. Prince Charming's back curled up as my hand made my way down to his tail.

"I agree," I whispered. "There is something fishy about Arabella Paxton."

Chapter Five

"Here ye, here ye," Faith Mortimer, the editor-in-chief—actually the only employee of the Whispering Falls Gazette—began the morning headlines.

The Gazette was the only paper in the community and the only way to subscribe was through having it delivered vocally. If you didn't subscribe, you didn't hear it. "There is going to be a grand celebration."

I picked up the charm and smiled knowing exactly what grand celebration Faith was talking about. Everyone knew what had happened with Oscar and his memory. They felt awful for me since I was grieving not only the fact Oscar wasn't allowed to live in Whispering Falls (since the rule was that you had to be a spiritualist to live here), but the fact that he didn't recall our relationship.

Lazily I picked up the ladle, slowly stirring the frothy potion and pictured a long veil over my head standing next to a tuxedo-clad Oscar Park. I slipped the tiny ring charm on the tip of my pinkie finger, not caring that I had let go of the ladle and once it was buried in the cauldron it would disintegrate. All I could do was pray Faith was talking about me.

Faith was Clairaudient spiritualist. She had the ability to hear things that were inaudible, beyond the normal realm of the human ears. Faith never knew exactly what was going to happen, she just knew it was going to.

"Keep in mind you have to break a few eggs to make an omelet," Faith continued with the headlines. Oscar and I had broken a lot of eggs in our past. Especially the time we had to send his uncle to jail after finding out he had not only killed Oscar's parents, but mine too. Thankfully he was rotting in a spiritualist jail cell, never to be heard of again.

"This announcement was brought to you by Glorybee Pet Shop. Be sure to tell Petunia Shrubwood you heard it in the Whispering Falls Gazette for a five percent discount on your next purchase. Remember, dust off those dancing shoes."

Sigh... The small gold circle was cutting off the circulation of the tip of my pinkie, turning it blue and cold. I poked the top of it a couple of times to watch the white dot disappear back to blue.

The shop door flew open, nearly causing me to jump out of my skin. Clearly this was not a good morning to be working on a potion as important as Oscar's.

"June Heal! June Heal!" Constance Karima rushed into the shop with her twin sister, Patience, closely behind her. I was ever so grateful Patience didn't escort her ostrich in with her. "You have got to make me a potion. I do not like omelets. I am lactose intolerant."

"Yep, lactose intolerant," Patience twitched behind her sister.

Behind her, through the window, I could see she had tied up her ostrich to one of the carriage lights. It pecked at dangling geraniums, eating every single red flower.

Poor thing, I glanced at the bald annuals that were so pretty just a few minutes ago.

"What are you talking about?" I put the charm next to the register and walked around to greet them.

The green-eyed twins were as tall as they were wide. They owned Two Sisters and a Funeral, the only funeral home in Whispering Hills, and perfect for them since they were Ghost Whisperer spiritualists.

Constance had her nose in every single detail of the paper, every single day. She didn't like Faith being in charge and she didn't like the fact that Faith didn't say who the headlines were for. That wasn't part of Faith's spiritual gift.

Patience. Poor Patience. She did very little for herself. She was rarely seen without Constance in front of her and she never spoke her mind. Only repeated the last few words of Constance's sentences. Sometimes I pictured myself shaking Patience and telling her to get a spine. She was only inflating Constance's ego by agreeing with everything she said.

"The news! June Heal, the news!" Constance wrung her hands and danced back and forth on her toes. Little did she know the headlines had to be about me. I ran my hands down my slender frame trying to decide on a flowing wedding dress or a more fitted mermaid type of dress. I had always seen myself as more of a traditional bride, but now that the time had come...I might have changed my mind.

"June? June, are you listening to me?" Constance snapped her thick, sausage fingers in my face, forcing me to jump out of my warm blissful daydream.

"Yes." I shook my head.

"I don't," Patience said.

"Don't what?" I asked.

"You weren't paying attention. I know." Patience tapped her temple.

"A...." my mouth dropped. "Patience?"

"Yes," she grinned. Her eyes squinted behind her wire-framed glasses. Her chubby fingers were nicely clasped in front of her, resting against her housedress.

"Did you forget I'm the Village President?" I asked.

"No, June, we didn't. That is why we are here. Did you hear the headlines?" Constance butted in, as she always did. "Something has to be done about those loose lips of that young spiritualist. They just blab and blab, making all the town folk worried to death. No wonder people are in here all day long getting sleep aids." She got closer, giving me the wonky eye. "Is that why you don't do something as the Village President? Are you using that poor girl, who is not a good spiritualist, for your financial gain?" Her eyes lowered.

"I'm sorry you feel that way." I smiled and tried to put on my best "I'm in charge hat" expression. "Faith is young. Don't you remember what it was like when you were young?"

"Are you saying I'm old?" Constance stood like a bull about to charge with her hands planted on her hips.

"No." I had to forcibly keep the smile on my lips. Dealing with these two was always a difficult but much needed task. "I'm just saying you have to give her time to grow into her own gift. We all were novice at one point and time."

"Do you think you are a pro?" She lifted her brow and stuck her chin up in the air giving me a good once-over.

Ignore her. There was a time when letting things fly right by you or right off your shoulders was a good time. This was one of those times.

She turned to her sister and said, "These kids today do not watch what they say nor do they care."

Constance was an old school spiritualist. She didn't like the young ones—like me and the Mortimer sisters—coming in and creating start-up businesses. Little did she realize that without us, Whispering Falls would die out. Plus we brought the younger customers and visitors to the community.

"You are Village President." Constance pointed between her and her sister. "That is why we came here. Don't you get the paper?"

"Yes. I get the paper." I looked at Constance and then changed my stare to Patience. Earlier when she had tapped her temple, confirming I was not listening to Constance ramble on about Faith's prediction and completely planning my wedding in my head, I realized she had been reading me. "But you." I pointed at Patience. "You broke Rule Number One."

"Don't be silly, June Heal." Constance grabbed Patience around the arm and pulled her close to her like I was going to snatch Patience up and put her in spiritualist jail. Too bad I didn't have the authority to just put people in a cell because I had a few people I would have loved to send there. Arabella Paxton was the first one who came to mind. "We are rule followers."

"Yes, rule followers," Patience repeated.

"Be sure you follow the rules," I warned and took both of them by the elbow. "It's time to get to work."

"Have a wonderful day." I smiled, pulling the door wide open for them. Wide open.

Gerald and Arabella were still standing in the middle of the street. Our eyes met. Immediately the two of them split up. Each going in the direction of their own shops.

"June Heal, you better get an editor, a real editor, for the Gazette before Faith sends all of us running for the woods!" Constance spoke faster when she saw that I was about to close the door.

Mewl, mewl. Mr. Prince Charming had left his perch and tangled himself between my legs. I bent down and picked him up. I rubbed his ear. "And you are going to be my man of honor."

"Puuuhleez." Madame Torres glowed from my bag that was hanging on the chair behind the counter.

"Ah oh." I let Mr. Prince Charming jump down from my arms and dart underneath one of the tables. "I forgot to get you out."

And damn it if she wasn't going to make me pay. She was the snarkiest crystal ball and I was the one who got stuck with her. I walked back to retrieve her from my bag and brought her to eye level.

"I'm sorry," I had to beg for forgiveness if I wanted to get my daily dose of hunk, I mean, daily dose of seeing what Oscar was up to. Remembering the geraniums, I grabbed a bottle from the counter. "Dew drop will work with a little dash of vermin."

I sat the dew drop on the counter and unscrewed the top before I added a couple sprinkles of vermin. With the lid screwed on tight, I shook the new potion up and headed back to the front door. "I'm wondering if I really have to get Oscar's memory potion made. Especially now with the impending celebration announcement."

I opened the front door and walked out through the gate to the bald geraniums. A little distance between me and Madame Torres was exactly what I needed before she said something awfully negative about Oscar and how I had been trying to come up with that potion to get his memory back.

I unscrewed the lid and squeezed the dropper ball top, bringing the potion up and filling the glass tube. "Here you go." Gently I let a couple of drops fall into the hanging basket. Before too long, the geraniums sprang back to life.

"There." I smiled and screwed the lid on before I headed back inside. "I've done my good deed for the day."

Before heading back into the shop, I stopped for a brief moment and looked over at Magical Moments. The line out the door made my stomach hurt. Secretly I had wished Arabella would not have any business and be forced to close shop. That was a farfetched idea. Who didn't love flowers?

"Hmmm." Madame Torres's displeasure was known when I walked back into the shop. I couldn't help but look back at her. Her pristine white face took up the entire glass ball. Her red lips looked like they were on fire. The purple eye shadow matched the purple turban and big purple jewel that was front and center on the perch of her head. Her eyes narrowed. "And you believe Faith Mortimer was talking about you and what's his name?"

"Oscar. Oscar Park. You know his name." I put the potion back on the shelf and walked back to the counter. "Who else could it be?" I sighed happily knowing I was about to be Mrs. Oscar Park. My cell chirped from the depths of my bag.

Madame Torres loved to rain on my parade. I didn't bother with her though. I'd put an umbrella up to shield off her big fat drops.

"See." I turned my phone around to show her Oscar had just texted me and asked me to have dinner with him tonight. "Tonight is going to be the night!"

"One little problem." Madame Torres had the voice...the negative voice.

"I don't want to know." I quickly texted him back about dinner and how I couldn't wait. "I own you. If I wanted to know your advice, I would ask."

"You can always show up to dinner a little late," Madame Torres warned me before she disappeared into the black abyss of the glass ball.

I glared at her. "What are you talking about?" I shook my head, knowing she was gone for a little while.

Ding, ding. The shop door opened. Our first customer of the day. I reached behind the counter to look at the cauldron to make sure it hadn't shut off. It was still rolling a slow boil.

"Good morning." I smiled and watched the woman head over to the table strictly for menopausal problems. I took a deep breath to clear my mind so I could read her vibe and let my intuition kick in to create exactly what she needed. My mind was all jumbled up with Oscar, the wedding, and grumpy Madame Torres.

"Yes." The woman appeared to be in her fifties. She had short blond hair, styled so cute with a little gel on top and sides as it was cut right above her ears where there was a fabulous pair of emerald teardrop earrings dangling down. "It is a marvy day."

Marvy?

"Just marvy," she said again, only this time I detected a hint of air in her voice. Kind of like the way wealthy people spoke.

"Let me know if I can help you with anything…" I watched to see what she was picking up because my intuition wasn't picking up on anything and that was the most important part of my job.

Whenever a customer walked through the door, I tapped into their intuition. This little spiritual gift allowed me to know exactly what potion to make for them. No evil magic here, only good stuff.

For instance, if a client came in for heartburn and they asked for a homeopathic heartburn medicine, I could tap into their soul and find out what was really bugging them. Maybe they were looking for love and that was causing the heartburn. I'd throw in a little love potion to the mix, send them home with a bottle, and it would cure them right up. Next thing I knew, the customer was right back in A Charming Cure with no more heartburn and a sweetie on their arm. *Cured.*

This woman was a different story. I grabbed my feather duster and dusted around the tables trying to get closer to her. Maybe the distance was the problem.

Sniff, sniff. I inched trying to get a whiff of something, anything that would give me a sense of what she was dealing with or what I was up against.

Nothing.

My sniffer and intuition was coming up short. And I didn't like it.

"Hrmph." I sighed.

"Are you okay?" The lady asked and walked closer to me. "You seem to be sniffing a lot. Do you have a cold?"

"I...," *ahem*, cleared my throat.

"It seems you have some lovely homeopathic remedies for a cold. Have you tried any of them?" She picked up the cold remedy bath salt with a pinch of Fly Aminta, which was good for opening the swollen airways due to the inflammation of the common cold.

"Allergies." I waved my hand in the air. "Of course I have tried all of my cures."

"Oh, you must be the owner of this lovely establishment." She grinned. Her eyes soften into a warm glow. She instantly made me miss Darla.

I glanced over at the picture hanging on the wall. The framed photo of me standing between my parents was my only photo of us. It was a gentle reminder of their love for me and it helped me get through the day.

"I am," I confirmed with pride. Darla would be so proud of me taking over A Dose of Darla and relocating to our hometown of Whispering Falls where I have tapped into my spiritual gift that I had gotten from my father's side of the family. Darla was not a spiritualist—far from it. She would catch something on fire and laugh, chalking it up to trial and error. "Are you looking for something specific?"

"Yes." She tapped her long fingers together before she adjusted the cowl-neck sweater, draping it a little more in the front. She smoothed the edges over her black leggings. Her slender legs ended in a pair of black flats. "I need something for a baby."

"Oh. I love babies." Images of a cute little bouncing baby boy who had big blue eyes like his dad, Oscar of course, and the black hair to match. Obviously the baby would have black hair since Oscar and I have black hair.

"Yes, well." The woman wasn't every entertained with my joy. "Do you have a little Luna Moth Wing?"

"Luna..." Okay, now she had my attention. How did she know about spiritualist ingredients?

"It's an old wives tale I Googled. It said some homeopathic stores sold such an ingredient." She perused the bottles on the special treatment shelf. That was the shelf that had a basic potion in each bottle and where I added the little touch of...magic.

"There is no such thing as Luna Moth Wing." Nervously I giggled and filed her comment in the back of my head.

Lately there had been so many customers coming into the shop with their own concoctions that it made me nervous. They said they were getting these on the Internet from a site of someone who said they were a homeopathic curist. The only real curists were in villages such as Whispering Falls and the public had no idea we truly existed.

"Oh really?" When she laughed, her cheeks balled up causing her eyes to dance. "My daughter told me that just because it's on the Internet doesn't mean it's true."

"You have a very smart daughter. I'm sure Dr. Google doesn't really exist." Oh, crap. I had to get on the Internet and see exactly what was going on. We, spiritualists, didn't really need the Internet. I, for one, had Madame Torres and the other spiritualists. But it wasn't a bad idea to look into. And I could use Oscar's computer before the proposal tonight. "So your daughter is the one who needs the potion?"

That had to be it. No wonder I wasn't able to read the woman's intuition. The potion wasn't for her.

"Between me and you…," the woman looked around to make sure no one was listening, but it was only me and her. "She is so upset about not getting pregnant that I think the stress is causing the issues." She put her finger in the corner of her eye and sniffled. "I've always wanted to be a grandmother."

"I couldn't agree more." I grabbed a tissue from off the counter and handed it to her. "The stress part." This was the point I knew I needed to help her and her daughter. This woman deserved to be a grandmother and I was going to help them. "Give me one second and I'll fix you something special to give to your daughter."

The woman slowly looked down at the floor and held her hands to her heart in gratitude.

I quickly got to work. I headed behind the partition on the other side of the counter. Tapping down the empty bottles on the shelf behind me, I waited until one lit up.

The special bottles had a tendency to know exactly what potion needed to go in it. A faint glow would tell me what bottle would be the best place to hold my future.

The purple heart-shaped bottle glowed with delight. I couldn't have been more pleased. I loved the delicate pink flowers etched in the center of the beautiful heart.

Carefully I held the bottle over top of the cauldron that held the beginning of Oscar's special potion and simply said, "Find your home." Like magic, the potion transferred from the cauldron into the bottle. I kissed the bottle lid before I screwed it on...tight. It never hurt to give something a little extra dose of love for good measure.

"I'll work on you later." I set it aside for when I had some down time. During the day it was hard for me to work on anything personal, due to the fact I was always creating for others. "Now." I dusted my hands off. "I've got to create a baby potion."

With the swipe of a cauldron cleaning cloth, the cauldron was ready to go. My customer would be a granny in no time.

"Are you crazy?" Madame Torres whispered from her glass ball.

"Shh," I warned her and put my finger up to my mouth. I bent down so she could hear me. "Are *you* crazy?" I asked sarcastically. "What if a customer hears you?"

"What if the Elders hear that you have used an ingredient on the 'do not use' list?"

"Do not use?" There was a list? A "do not use" list? I shuddered to think of what else could be on the list. There was nothing in my shop that I hadn't used before. If there was some sort of "do not use" ingredient, surely I would have known it by now. "If it was 'do not use,' KJ would have told me."

I had no idea how I got appointed to be the new Village President, but revisiting the by-laws was the first order of business at the next meeting.

I glanced at the calendar when I reached over to get some Snowberries to start the potion. "Meeting" was printed big on today's date. Dang! The big engagement was going to have to wait.

Someone tell me why I had agreed to be the Village President? I groaned and grabbed a handful of Snowberries and threw them in the cauldron. I watched them swirl around and around until the small round berry turned into a yellow stream before it exploded into a frothy sapphire tonic.

Since I didn't know the woman's daughter, I wasn't able to read items she loved to eat, which was part of the intuition thing I had going on. I could disguise any potion with a food smell or taste to make sure they took the cure created for them.

Snowberries were the sweetest berry around. "Normal" people wouldn't have access to the Snowberries since it was only available to the spiritual community. Those little secrets were how we had kept the economy up in Whispering Falls while the rest of the surrounding cities struggled. Regardless, everyone loved Snowberries because the sweet taste took on the flavor of the recipient's current craving.

"When are you going to be seeing your daughter?" I made idle chitchat to pass the time.

"Not for a couple of weeks," the woman responded.

The ding, ding of the bell was followed up by a voice. "Delivery!" the voice shouted into the shop.

I peeked my head around the partition. There was a boy with a baseball cap on standing in the doorway of the shop with a bouquet of fresh-cut wildflowers in his arms.

"Whoa!" His mouth and hands dropped down at the same time. He held the flowers by the stems. "What kind of place is this?"

I turned the cauldron on low and brushed my hands off as I hurried over to get the flowers.

"Welcome to A Charming Cure. This is a homeopathic cure shop. Are those for me?" I squealed. The customer moseyed up next to the counter and looked at the flowers.

"Those are beautiful." She smiled.

"Are you June Heal?" the delivery boy asked.

"I am," I nodded. The only thing better than getting flowers from Oscar, was a kiss from Oscar.

"Then they are for you." He handed the flowers to me.

Instantly I held them to my nose and inhaled. Late Purple Aster, White Avens, Arrowleaf, White Baneberry, Shrub Yellowroot, French Mulberry, Tickseed Sunflower, and many types of greenery I couldn't name were all bundled in a burlap tie. It was the most beautiful assortment I had ever seen.

"Where is the card?" I wanted to know who they were from.

"No card." He shrugged.

"What?" I laughed, thinking he was joking. He didn't crack a smile. "You are joking right?"

"Nope. No card. Coolio place though." He cocked his lips to the side and nodded looking around the shop.

"Thanks." I wasn't sure if coolio was a word but it must be for the younger kids today. Not that I was old. Twenty-eight still seemed young to me. But I wasn't around many young people, so coolio it was.

"I've got to get back to work." I held the flowers close to me. The customer smiled and went back to looking around while I went back to the cauldron and the delivery boy left.

The flowers lingered on my mind and the vision of Oscar and Arabella standing next to his car popped into my head.

"That's what he was doing," I whispered and reached over to touch them.

Sneaky devil. He had been giving Arabella a flower order for me. It had to be. He was doing a great job for prepping me for tonight, even though I was going to have to rearrange my plans since I had completely forgotten about the village meeting.

Suddenly my head started to swirl, like it always did when my potion intuition was about to kick in. It wasn't a smell but a vision. A vision of a piece of greenery with small pink berries growing on the stem.

Had I tapped into the customer's sense of what needed to go into her daughter's special cure for her baby-making problem?

"Hmm." I grabbed a vase from underneath the counter to stick the flowers in so they would live until I was able to properly display them and it jumped out at me like an angry frog.

In the bundle of wildflowers was one stem of the greenery I had a vision of. Without thinking, I plucked a couple off and threw it in the cauldron.

Mixing the greenery in with the Snowberries, the potion surged into a whirlpool of pumpkin color with a hint of amber. It was beautiful to watch as I mixed more and more ingredients.

"And for the final touch." I grinned and turned around to get a pinch of Bleeding Crown Root and a tad bit of Luna Moth Wing. With the last toss, I said, "Let's get it on."

Okay, so I didn't have a good cure chant for baby-making, but a little Marvin Gaye seemed to work for a lot of people and the cure because it rolled into a steaming pulsating elixir that looked good enough to lick the sides of the cauldron.

"I'm almost done," I called out to the woman.

"Take your time because this is our last hope." There was a little bit of relief in her voice, but not much. "You are our last hope."

It wasn't like I was a doctor and I certainly wasn't God, but it was great that I could put some hope into people's lives.

Before I even touched a bottle to see which one was for the cure, a bottle was already glowing when I turned around.

I smiled. I had known the crystal hourglass bottle with the gold molding around the base with the delicate gold flowers etched in the glass was going to hold a special potion. What was more special than a baby?

"Perfect," the word left my lips in a whisper.

"Are you sure you want to do this cure?" Madame Torres appeared. Her lashes were heavy with black mascara, black liner rimmed her lids.

"Shh!" I put my finger up to my lip and held the bottle over the cauldron. Little sparks flew up in the air, sending a little fireworks show right below my fingertips. I leaned back so my eyes wouldn't get caught in the beautiful display of colors shooting out of the cauldron.

"Is everything okay back there?" the woman called out.

"Perfect!" I called back to her and watched the mixture get sucked up into the bottle before the cauldron shut off. "Perfect. " I held the beautiful crystal bottle up to get a good look at my creation.

Proudly I walked around the partition and sat the bottle on the counter.

"All done?" the woman asked.

"All done." I pushed the bottle to the edge of the counter for her to get a look at before quickly pulling them away. The bottle had heated up and burnt the tip of my pinkie finger. "And the bottle is just so lovely. I'm sure your daughter will love it." I drew my hand to my eyes and noticed the small burn.

I quickly jotted down the directions and added up the cost, ignoring my pinkie pain. Sometimes reactions were unexplainable even if everything did go well.

With the exchange of money and wishes of good luck, the customer was happily on her way out the door when a loud scream pelted through the open door followed up by someone screaming "yes" over and over.

"Yes! Yes! Yes!" Petunia Shrubwood jumped up and down. Her floppy up-do hairstyle bounced up and down, sending birds flying out as fast as she bounced. My neck was getting a work out by moving up and down watching her bounce around. She was obviously having some sort of spell because she would never hurt the animals that nested in that hairstyle she had, nor would she hurt Gerald who was crouched down in front of her looking like he was scared to death.

Gerald Regiula was a saint because I didn't know a man who would put up with a woman who was as obsessed with animals as Petunia was.

"Yes! I will marry you!" She stopped bouncing. My heart stopped.

I could see a faint smile growing underneath his top hat before he flipped it off and jumped up grabbing her into his arms and flying her around like they were playing maypole.

Everyone was there. Raven and Faith stood under the Wicked Good awning, Ophelia and Colton held hands on the front porch of Ever After Books, Isadora Solstice stood on the steps of Mystic Lights. I scanned down the street and could see Bella Van Lou smiling from the front of Bella's Baubles. I waited to see the ring he gave her, but he seemed to forget that little detail.

"Oh! A Whispering Falls wedding." Chandra Shango stood next to me with a spark in her eyes as she watched Gerald and Petunia free floating in the street, not a care in the world. "I had a feeling with the Gazette headlines that there was going to be a wedding. I love weddings."

I gulped and looked over at Chandra. She had on a red cloak with yellow stars all over it making the blue jewel in the middle of her turban stand out. Her long dangling gold earrings made the outfit.

"Are you okay, dear?" Chandra patted my arm. I was known for fainting in times of a crisis and this was a crisis. At least in my world.

"Isn't this lovely?" Arabella yelled over to us. My eyes held hers too long. She smiled. Blankly I stared.

"June?" Chandra waved her hands in front of me. Slowly I turned my face toward hers. I tried to focus on her bright red fingernails as they waved in front of my face. "I don't think you are okay." She got closer.

Then the darkness set in.

Chapter Six

"She can't ever let anyone have a happy moment. She takes center stage every single time by doing her little fainting spell." The angry voice rang in my ears as I came to. "See. Everyone is texting everyone asking if *June Heal* is okay. Not a bit concerned about me, *the bride*."

I didn't have to open my eyes to know it was Petunia Shrubwood talking. Of course she was angry with me for fainting during the biggest moment of her life which was supposed to be the biggest moment of my life. Her engagement, not mine.

"Oh dear." The nervous quiet voice came from Mary Lynn.

What was she doing there? I took advantage of my fainting spell and kept my eyes closed. Even though I did pass out, I still hadn't processed the idea that Faith's premonition had been about Petunia and Gerald.

"Now everyone is going to ask her about her fainting spell and not about my engagement. This day will forever be tainted with a June Heal fainting spell, just like all the other times." Petunia was angry. I had seen her angry and it was not a good sight. "I can just see it now. We will be around the Gathering Rock for the meeting and she will hog all the attention. It's not enough that she's young and beautiful too."

"Calm down," Isadora Solstice said in a reasoning voice.

"I don't blame you for being upset."

Arabella? I lifted my eyelid just enough to see Arabella Paxton standing at my feet picking her nails. Mr. Prince Charming jumped on my chest, nearly causing me to blow my cover. He kneaded my stomach with his front paws, purring the whole time.

"She does seem to be a little needy. At least it looked that way when she got her panties in a wad when her friend...um..." She tapped her temple like she couldn't remember Oscar's name, but I knew better. "Os...," she hesitated.

"Oscar," Mary Lynn finished her sentence.

It took every ounce of my spiritual soul not to jump up and rip out Arabella's spiritual soul.

"Now, now." Isadora, Izzy for short, put her palm on my forehead. "He did love her or he wouldn't have denounced his spiritual heritage to save her life."

I could always count on Izzy to be on my side. After all, she was the reason I moved to Whispering Falls. She knew I was a spiritualist before *I* knew I was a spiritualist. She came to visit me in Locust Grove and suggested I move A Dose of Darla to Whispering Falls. It was the best decision I had ever made.

"She can't help that she faints." Izzy knew my fainting spells were caused by something other than low blood sugar or something medical. She knew there had to be an underlying intuition vision. Only I didn't know what that vision was. I just knew that the engagement between Petunia and Gerald was plagued. Plagued by *what* was the question and one I was going to have to figure out.

"Did he?" Arabella drummed her fingers together. "I mean, he isn't a spiritualist?"

She knew darn well he was no longer a spiritualist.

Cough, cough, cough. I faked with my eyes still closed. Mr. Prince Charming wasn't buying my act. He knew me too well. He swiped my cheek with the pad of his paw.

"Stop," I whispered and blew a stream of air out of my mouth to make him move. He didn't budge. *Damn cat.*

This was one of those moments I wished Oscar hadn't made the deal with the Elders and he still had his memory. He'd be right there by my side and let little Miss Fresh Flowers know she was *way* out of line.

"Stop talking. She's coming to," Izzy warned. The swoosh of her A-line skirt filled the air as she bent down and got closer to my ear. "June dear."

"What happened?" I pretended to not remember the whole entire conversation or engagement. *If only.* I really didn't want to remember. I wanted to remember the feeling I had when I truly thought the vision was going to be me. Me and Oscar. How stupid was I?

Oscar and I hadn't even gotten back together since he lost his memory, though he did know about my spiritual gift and how Eloise was his aunt.

"I can tell you what happened." An angry Petunia stepped into my vision. To take it like a man, I propped myself up on my elbows ready for the blow. I had ruined the happiest moment of her life. I deserved what I had coming to me. "You, June Heal, have ruined my proposal!"

"I…" I sat up but Izzy put a hand on my shoulder to stop me.

"Petunia, you stop that." Izzy gave her a stern warning.

"Stop what? The truth?" Arabella asked. She obviously didn't know the protocol around here and I was all too eager to teach her by escorting her right out of town.

Petunia planted her fists on each side of her swirly hips and nodded her head agreeing with Arabella. Petunia's floor length black skirt hung like a pair of drapes over her hips and it didn't help her shape with the scoop neck shirt tucked into the waist band. "She asked what happened and I'm going to tell her." She shook her fist at me before she pointed to Arabella. "Well, she's going to tell her."

"You can't stand to see someone in love now that you have lost Oscar and you don't want her to be happy." There was an evil twinkle in Arabella's gorgeous eyes. She made evil look beautiful.

"Me?" I jumped up, knocking Izzy almost to the ground. "I changed the by-laws for you and Gerald." I ignored Arabella and spoke straight to Petunia.

"For me?" She cackled out loud. She poked my chest with her finger. "You liar! That was for you and Oscar. He was the sheriff and you are the owner of A Charming Cure which meant you couldn't be together."

Damn. She was half right. When I first moved to Whispering Falls, Rule Number Three stated that you couldn't have more than one shop in the family. I had no idea why that rule was in place, but it was stupid. Especially since I wanted Oscar and the rules prevented me from it. I had also known that Gerald and Petunia were secretly dating, which I told no one, and when I became Village President, I knew it was going to be the first rule I was going to amend. Now that it was on the table, we would take a final vote at the next meeting.

"That is not true." Okay, half true. "I want you and Gerald to be together. You two love each other. Besides, it's a silly rule."

"Yes we do love each other and you of all people should be happy for us." She stomped her foot. Her messy up-do tilted to the right. A small chipmunk held on for dear life before it scurried back into the mop-top of hair piled high on her head. "And God knows we have waited a long time to get married."

She was right on that too. Each of them had to be in their late fifties and neither of them had been married.

"You took the Presidency away from me and now my engagement." For a minute I thought she was going to hit me. "What else do you want? My pet shop? My bees? My life?"

Arabella nodded right alongside of Petunia, giving Petunia the courage she needed to slam me.

Oh no. I was in big trouble. She was never going to let me live down the whole Village President situation. It wasn't like I had campaigned to be in charge. It wasn't like I moved to Whispering Falls and craved to be the leader. I wanted to open my homeopathic cure shop and live happily ever after with Oscar by my side. So far, it's been far from happily ever after.

Petunia had always wanted to be in charge when Izzy stepped down and that was how it might work in a normal election. Whispering Falls was far from normal and so was the way a new president took office. I was appointed and didn't have a real choice in the matter.

"I'm beyond happy for you. Thrilled in fact. I want to give you a bridal shower." *Bridal shower?* Where that had come from I had no idea, but by the look on her face, it was brilliant. I continued to feed on her expressions. "With cake, tea, presents for the happy couple, and lots of decorations."

"What?" Arabella's mouth dropped. By the look on her face, she knew I had just played a trump card.

I had never even thrown a birthday party or any type of party. I didn't even know where to begin to throw a bridal shower. I would make a stop to Ever After. I was sure there were manuals on bridal showers.

"Do you mean it?" Petunia's face softened and so did her shoulders. Her brown eyes held a tear in the corner. She blinked. The tear rolled down her cheek and dripped onto the floor. I nodded. "You are happy for me."

"I am." My insides ached as I confirmed how happy I was that she had gotten engaged and I wasn't. The thought of going through bridal shower manuals made me sick to my stomach. But I put on a happy smile. It wasn't that I wasn't happy for them. I would be really, really happy for them if I was engaged too, but I wasn't. Not yet. It could happen. But my intuition didn't alert me that something great was going to happen. It alerted me that something bad, something very bad was going to happen.

"I'll supply all the flowers for your shower." Arabella curled up on her toes and jabbed her finger in the air. Her voice escalated, "And I'll do the wedding too."

"That settles it." Petunia clasped her hands to her mouth. I noticed she didn't have a ring on her left hand yet, reminding me of the dove and ring charm Mr. Prince Charming had given me.

What did that charm mean? Faith's words rang in my head from this morning's headlines, *you have to break a few eggs to make an omelet.* Faith's second part of her prediction popped into my head. What did that mean? More importantly, what did that mean in terms of a celebration?

Yes. I would keep the bride and the flower girl close to my side and make sure nothing went wrong. Especially with the flower girl.

"Then we must get planning." She curled her hand around my elbow and the other hand around Arabella's. She drew us close to her. I looked over at Izzy.

Izzy pushed her long blond wavy hair from around her face. She winked one of her big hazel eyes at me. She understood the position I was in and how carefully I had to play my cards.

As the Village President before me, I had seen Izzy get into some very compromising positions. With complete care and caution, I had seen her get out of those positions unscathed, happy and keeping Whispering Falls running without a hitch.

"Yes." I patted Petunia's hand, ignoring Mr. Prince Charming's figure eights and Arabella's stares. "Let's get started. But first," I pulled the charm bracelet out of my pocket and the new charm from Mr. Prince Charming, "can we stop by Bella's Baubles? I need to drop off my bracelet."

Chapter Seven

"I wondered when you were going to get down here,"
Bella Van Lou was hunched over the glass jewelry case
with an eye loupe tucked into a squinted eye. Her long
blond hair cascaded over her shoulder landing in a pool of
strands on top of the glass. Her cheeks balled up when she
smiled, exposing the gap between her two front teeth. She
stood straight, all five-foot-two of her. "We must get that
charm on your bracelet."

"You're telling me." I rolled my eyes and shut the door
behind me. Normally Bella's Baubles was packed, and
today I was thankful it wasn't. Everyone loved to come in
and look at the unique gemstones she sold there plus the
advice she gave every customer who walked in. She was
the town astrologer. She knew exactly what piece of
jewelry was perfect for anyone who stepped foot in her
shop. I needed her advice today.

She stood up and took the loupe out of her eye. It was
attached to a long gold chain; the glass magnifier was
incased in a frame of a swan—the glass being the body. "I
can only imagine how you felt about the big proposal
news."

"It's fine." I didn't know why I even tried to cover up
the fact that I was hurt. Bella knew everything about me.
She knew everything about Oscar. Not that she read our
stars, but I had told her. She was the first person I had
confided in when I moved to Whispering Falls.

"June." The mothering, reasoning voice of Bella was
about to give me a pity lecture. "I saw you faint. At that
moment I knew you were upset. Even when I heard the
headlines I knew you were going to think it was you who
was celebrating. Your time will come."

I held in the outward cry and sobs I would later do in my pillow. I bit my lip to forget the heart pain and focused on the pain in my mouth of my teeth gnawing down.

"Your time is not now." She picked up a beautiful ruby and rubbed it with the cleaning cloth. "So, do you want me to explain the charm?"

"The charm." I had forgotten to take it out of my pocket. I pulled it out and laid the charm and my bracelet on the glass case. "Yes. This made me think the headline was about me."

As much as I wanted to drop it, I just couldn't let it go.

"It's only natural since Oscar has embraced your spiritual heritage." Bella put the ruby gently on the cloth and moved around the counter.

"He has a lot more questions, but the last time we talked," I took a deep breath, "he asked more questions. He laughed when he realized I had sabotaged his date with Annie and he didn't care." I smiled like a teenager. "He even said that he knew there was something special between us. He said it was in his bones."

"See. Give it time." She rubbed her jeweled fingers up and down the side of my arm in a comforting way. Only it wasn't all that comforting. It really kind of hurt when the rings would catch my skin, pinching it. "Let your relationship grow into something special. You two will be like your parents."

"Oh. Lovely just lovely." Arabella stood at the open shop door. She ran her hands down the ornamental door that made Bella's Baubles fun to step into. Bella had the door specially made with sparkly gemstones inset in the wood grain. It was amazing, but even more fascinating when the sun directly hit it. "The first time I visited Whispering Falls, your shop door caught my eye."

Arabella stepped into the shop. She slid her long finger along the glass counters, eyeing the jewelry. She stopped where I was standing, near the engagement rings.

"You must be Arabella Paxton." Bella put her hand out. "I'm Bella Van Lou. It's my pleasure to finally meet you since I've heard so many great things about your fancy floral designs. I must stop in and take a look for myself."

"Oh June, have you been telling stories about me?" Arabella's ice-blue eyes twinkled like the aquamarine stone glistening right underneath her hand in the glass counter.

"I'd never do such a thing." I laughed trying to give my best "I don't give a shit about you" impression.

"Oh no." Bella pulled back and crossed her arms. "June is the finest citizen around here. Did you know she's the Village President?"

"I did." Arabella smiled. "And that keeps her from idle gossip? Isn't everyone in town always curious when a new resident moves in? Especially with a new shop?"

"You two talk as if I'm not here." Curious or not, I didn't like her and I wish my gut or intuition would give me some insight on her but it was silent. "Arabella, we are delighted to have you here." Another lie.

"What are you two ladies looking at?" Her eyes drew down. "Engagement rings?"

"I was just saying how much I loved that one." I pointed to the simple vintage engagement ring. The platinum ring was one of my favorites and Bella knew it was the one I wanted when Oscar and I were dating. Once Bella had told me it was from the 1910's, I was sold. "I love how simple the stone is. Just one stone."

"Don't you think it's a little plain?" Arabella quipped.

"Plain?" I shook my head. "Perfect. Listen," I turned toward her, "I would take a bread tie if Osc—" I stopped myself when I realized who I was talking to.

She was definitely charming, manipulating the situation, making me forget about her little rendezvous with my man.

"What can I do for you?" Bella interrupted when she could see I was struggling.

"Nothing." Arabella looked back at *my* ring as she drummed her fingertips together. "Just wanted to introduce myself. I must go before my grandmother gives the shop away."

Before we knew it, Arabella was gone.

"She brought her grandmother too?" Bella grabbed the Windex from behind the counter and removed the evidence of Arabella's fingerprints.

"Her grandmother is Mary Lynn." My eyes rose.

"No way!" Bella eyes and mouth shot open. This was probably the first time any of the Elders had shared anything personal with anyone. "I wonder if your mom and dad knew her family? You know, your mother would have loved that ring too." She winked and took the ring from the case. She used her gem cleaning cloth to give it a once-over before she handed it to me.

I couldn't help myself. I stuck it right on my left ring finger. Just to see how it felt. I wasn't going to lie. It felt and looked good.

It was true; Darla would have loved this ring. My parents were in love. Darla was not a spiritualist and Dad was. I had no idea how they met. Eloise Sandlewood, Oscar's aunt, was Darla's best friend. I really did need to find out. They were proof that a spiritualist and a non-spiritualist could get married and live happily.

"One day." I slid the ring off my finger and gently placed it back on the counter. "Thanks. I've got to run." I pointed toward the door. "I'm meeting Petunia at Ever

After so we can look at bridal shower things. First I have to go over to talk to Faith about her headlines."

"Karimas?" Bella was not blind to the sisters' rants and raves. Which were about pretty much everything.

"And…" I let out a deep sigh. "I have an apology to make to Gerald after that."

"Aww. Yes I suppose you do. I'll let you know when your charm bracelet is ready." She reached over and picked up my bracelet, dangling it from her fingertips. "And June," she stopped right before I opened the door to leave, "don't worry about Arabella Paxton."

Hhmph. Without answering I stepped out of the shop and stood on the steps of Bella's Baubles. Whispering Falls was beautiful and not even Arabella Paxton was going to ruin that.

It was as though someone came in and carved the town into the side of a mountain. The moss-covered cottage shops were nestled deep in the woods, and had the most beautiful entrances I'd ever seen.

Each shop had a colorful awning, displaying its name over the top of the ornamental gated doors. It had a magical feel. Seeing A Charming Cure's awning flapping in the wind filled me with a warm fuzzy. If only Oscar were here, my life would be complete.

I turned around and admired Bella's Baubles. A quaint cream cottage with a pink wood door that was adorned with different colored jewels. A perfect match to Bella.

Izzy caught my attention as she slipped into Mystic Lights, the shop she owned. She must have left the group of gaggling women who had stood over me when I was out cold. I couldn't help but wonder what they had said about me when I had left. None of them seemed to be too happy with me.

The outside of Mystic Lights was amazing and mystic. The hunter-green wood door was encased in the most beautiful stone archway. The heavy black metal door handles added to the old world charm. It definitely fit Izzy's personality.

Across the street from Bella's Baubles was Wicked Good Bakery. The striped blue and pink awning hanging just above the hot pink ornamental wooden door was a perfect choice and fit the Mortimer sisters to a tee.

I closed my eyes and enjoyed the timeless smells of the baked goods inside that wrapped around me like a warm blanket letting me momentarily forget why I had to make a stop to see Faith.

Petunia would be fine for a few more minutes in Ever After waiting on me. She was probably drowning in disgusting blissful happiness, surrounded by piles of books about weddings and all things frilly, white, and related to her big day. I'd even bet Arabella was all over Petunia and had even run to her store to get samples. That girl was on a mission to one-up me on anything I was going to do...*ever.*

Inwardly I groaned secretly wishing it was me flipping through wedding planners, thinking about making decisions like: shoes, cream or white dress, tiered cakes, tiara versus veil. Decisions, decisions, happy decisions. *Sigh.*

I hurried across the street and opened the door to Wicked Good. I pushed my way past the customers and headed to the front of the line. Raven was behind the counter putting fresh scones in the glass case. Faith was sweeping up the floor around the café tables.

The inside of Wicked Good made me feel like a little girl again.

The lime green walls looked amazing against the jars of candy that lined them. The cake stands on each table had the most amazing assortment of cupcakes I'd ever seen.

The black-and-white checkered floor led the way to a room filled with Victorian-style dining furniture.

"Hey, June." Faith was very exotic looking with her long blond hair and onyx eyes. Her nails were always perfectly manicured in the deepest of pinks. Her clothes were the latest trends and she dressed to impress. I swear her long lashes made a swoosh sound when she batted them they were so long. "Let me get you a cupcake. Special today." She rubbed her tummy and lifted her brows along with a big smile but not before rearranging a few pale-pink flowers in an etched-glass vase. "Have you ever seen cherry blossoms arranged in a bouquet?" Faith shook her head with a happy smile across her face. "That Arabella is awesome at her job."

"*Awesome.*" I rolled my eyes and looked at the cupcakes. "Sure, I could use a cupcake." How could I resist? When the world had taken my all-time favorite snack, Ding Dongs, out of circulation, Raven did her best to imitate them with her own creation she called June's Gems, affectionately named after me. Even now that Ding Dongs were back on the market, I stuck with June's Gems. "I could eat all the cupcakes in the place right now."

"Oh," Faith's lips pursed. Her brows wrinkled in worry. "You want to sit while I grab you one?"

I nodded and took a seat at one of the open tables. The crowd seemed to be piling in more and more. Once the Piggly Wiggly in Locust Grove started to carry some of Wicked Good's items in their pastry section of the grocery store, the residents started to venture through the curvy back roads and deep into the woods to find Whispering Falls so they could stockpile on their favorite desserts. Who could resist a hot muffin, scone, or dessert of choice—hot and right out of the oven? Plus it helped business with the other shops. Since Ever After Books was our newest shop in town, I was hoping it would also draw new customers.

"Okay," Faith saddled up to the table carrying a tray with two coffees and two cupcakes. She sat a cup in front of me and placed a chocolate cupcake covered with fudge ganache frosting with a small fondant red heart adorned by white sprinkles that had fallen in just the right place.

"How fitting." I took the heart off the top. There was a small crack that ran down the middle. No wonder Faith brought it to me. Raven would never have a crack in her creations. She generally donated the rejects, but today I must be the charity case so I plopped it in my mouth. Crack or not, it was yummy.

Faith sat in the chair across from me, her hands flailing in the air like she was fanning the air and said, "I heard you were having some heart issues." She gave a martyred sigh. "You know. The voices," referring to her spiritual gift.

"They are right." I bit into the delish deep chocolate goodness and let my mind get lost for a moment before Faith broke the silence. "And Arabella isn't helping either."

"Really?" Faith shrugged. "I found her charming."

"She's very charming to Oscar." I brushed off the notion of Arabella and Oscar. Faith didn't need to know my problems and I wasn't here to solve them. I was here to solve how she reported the news. "Though it's probably just her personality," I lied.

"I guess you are bummed about the headlines?" Faith and Raven knew all about me and Oscar. Since they moved to Whispering Falls, they had been my closest allies. We are all the same age and had met at Hidden Halls, A Spiritualist University. Faith and I were in the same Intuition Class that Eloise taught. Our relationship was a little rocky, but once we got to know each other, we had become fast friends.

"Bummed isn't the word for it." An instant lump in my throat told me I was about to cry.

Faith reached over the table. "Please don't be upset. From what I understand Oscar is coming around to the whole 'witch' thing." We laughed.

It was true. Oscar didn't get the world spiritual. He said from what I had described, it was all witchy like. To us, witchy was a negative term and implied evil. Whispering Falls and its residents were none of those things. We only brought good and happiness to everyone, not evil or bad.

"He is and we are moving forward. Slowly." I eyed Faith's cupcake that she hadn't even touched. She pushed it toward me. I took it without even thinking about the calorie intake I would later regret. "Thanks."

"I knew you were going to need another one." She winked. "But your time is coming. How do we not know that the headlines didn't mean two celebrations?"

"Does it?" My spirit felt a little tug of possibilities.

"I don't know." Faith shrugged. "I just read it as I get it. The chance of it is there. What can I do to help you?"

"Do you know what you meant by breaking a few eggs to make an omelet?" I was trying to come up with a way to talk to her about the way she reports what she heard, but the one line still bugged me.

"I don't know what that meant. Like I said, I say it as it comes to me. Part of the job. In fact," she planted her elbows on the table and leaned forward, "I almost didn't report that because I knew it would send the Karima sisters into flames. But I did what I'm supposed to do." She got up. "I've got to get back to work before Raven fires me."

"Hey," I grabbed her hand stopping her before she got away. "I'm going to have a bridal shower for Petunia. Do you think y'all could do the treats for the party?"

"Good for you. That's nice to do." She squeezed my hand. "Here comes Raven, I'm sure she'd love to."

"What's up?" Raven rubbed her hands off on her apron with the big Wicked Good logo printed on the front of it. Her coal-black hair was pulled into a low side ponytail and dangling over her right shoulder.

"I was here to get the scoop on the headlines." I finished off my second cupcake. "Delish." I rubbed the chocolate from the corners of my mouth. I rubbed my empty wrist. It was rare that I didn't wear my bracelet. And without it not only did I feel naked, but unprotected.

"Yeah, about those." She pointed to the cupcakes. "I knew you'd be here."

I pounded my forehead with the palm of my hand. This was not good. Raven was an Aleuromancy spiritualist. She found answers and messages baked in dough.

"I'm sorry." She reached over like Faith had done and grabbed my hands. She rubbed them. Not one bit comforting me. It made me feel worse.

"Go on," I encouraged her. "I know there is a message. Good or bad, throw it on me."

There wasn't much more I was going to be able to take.

"I'm not sure what the real message is, but every time I made one of those damn hearts, it would crack right down the middle."

"I saw the crack but thought it was a reject cupcake." I groaned and tried to rub out the ache pulsating through my chest. "How do you know it was about me?"

"You aren't going to put me in jail are you?" Raven referred to Rule Number One—spiritualists cannot read other spiritualists.

"Are you kidding?" I drew back with my hands planted on my chest. "My life, Oscar, my future is relying on your message."

"I don't know about all of that, but I do know that it doesn't involve Oscar," her voice trailed off.

"What do you mean?" There wasn't any other guy I was interested in…ever.

"Clearly it was about you and your shop, but someone who is heavily involved with Petunia." Raven peered over my shoulder. Faith was behind the counter waving her over. The line had grown twice the size since I had gotten there. "I've gotta go."

Raven jumped up.

"Oh! I can do the bridal shower treats," she said over the crowd. "It was in the dough." She lifted her hands in the air.

Chapter Eight

In the dough.

That didn't make me feel any better. Granted I didn't know a ton about Petunia, but I did know a few things. And one of those things was Arabella Paxton. She was new and she already proved to dislike me, not to mention she was trying to get her hooks in Petunia and Gerald's wedding.

"June," Gerald tipped his hat when I walked past The Gathering Grove on my way back to A Charming Cure. He was outside serving tea to the customers sitting at the wrought iron tables underneath the store's awning. "Petunia said to tell you that she was going to have to meet you after work. There was a line of customers outside of Glorybee and she was sure someone was going to adopt Clyde."

"Oh darn," I quipped. "I was really hoping to get some items crossed off your wedding list."

"About that." Gerald rubbed his hands over his mustache and twirled the end on one side. "You have been an awful good sport about all of this."

"Oh," I brushed it off even though my heart was breaking like the little heart on the cupcakes I had just gulped down in my time of sorrow. Suddenly my stomach felt sick. "I'm super happy for you and the village. A strong power couple."

"I know you told Oscar about all of this." He waved his hand in the air referring to the magic that lies in Whispering Falls. "I understand he is taking it very well."

I nodded. "He is. Eloise is doing a great job showing him pictures of his past with his family." I crossed my fingers and held them up in the air. "I'm truly grateful to have been able to keep the best friend I have known all my life. That's enough for me."

Disconcerted, Gerald crossed his arms and pointedly looked away.

"What?" I asked. There was definitely something he was keeping from me.

Suddenly he straightened up. *Ahem*, he cleared his throat, *"Nothing."*

I followed his gaze. Arabella stood on the steps of her shop pretending to adjust the flowers on the mannequin skirt.

"Have you met our newest shop owner?" It was a perfect time to question him about me seeing them standing in the street earlier—much earlier than when he had proposed to Petunia.

"Petunia informs me she is a nice woman." Gerald tipped his top hat, hiding his eyes from the sudden burst of sun shooting from the sky.

"I saw the two of you talking earlier. Do you know her from somewhere?"

"No." He gave me a narrowed glinting glance.

I chewed on my lower lip and stole a look at him. Once again, he was looking at Arabella and she was looking back at him.

"Really?" My gut tugged, my intuition waved a red flag. "You don't know her?" I looked back at Arabella. When our eyes met, she darted into her shop.

"I've got to get back to work." Gerald patted the top of his top hat before he tilted his head and dismissed himself and my question.

"*Great.*" Unfamiliar sounds seeped into my soul. There was something to Gerald and Arabella's little morning chat and my gut told me I was going to have to get to the bottom of it, regardless of her interest in Oscar.

I glared at Magical Moments with burning, reproachful eyes as I made my way down to A Charming Cure. The chatter outside of Glorybee caught my attention. The line was ten people deep.

They were all oohing and awing over Clyde who was on his perch in the window of the shop. Petunia was happily grooming him. He knew he was on display. His chest was puffed out and one of his legs stretched to the side as his tail feathers spread apart. Petunia's face was bright with pride.

Clyde was a big macaw bird that gave his opinion whether you wanted to hear it or not. Petunia was able to talk to animals which made her the perfect owner of Glorybee Pet Shop. She was a natural with animals and when Mr. Prince Charming wasn't around, I knew he was hanging out with Petunia.

Clyde. He was a different story. No matter how much Petunia complained about the old bird, she loved him to the core. I highly doubted she was going to let someone adopt him. She was all talk. Just like she was all talk when she refused to admit she and Gerald were a couple.

"Hi everyone." I walked to the front of Glorybee and tapped on the window before I headed over to A Charming Cure.

Petunia waved and Clyde nodded his head up and down.

"Thank you," Petunia mouthed and pointed to a beautiful bouquet of yellow orchids. She put her hands to her chest. "I love them."

I smiled not knowing what she was talking about. I bet her new best friend, Arabella, had given them to her.

I might be a little biased, but A Charming Cure was the prettiest shop in Whispering Falls. I reached over and plucked a couple of stray vines away from the two front windows; the rest of the outside was covered in the most beautiful wisteria vine. The purple and white flowers grew up and around the front door. "Give me a minute to open back up," I told a customer who was waiting for the shop to open.

This morning after my fainting spell, Izzy was good enough to close A Charming Cure so I could get back on my feet. And since Petunia wasn't able to meet up, there was no reason I couldn't open for the rest of the day. It was still early and there were a lot of customers.

Quickly I rushed through the shop, turning on all the little table lights, illuminating the inside. I flipped on my cauldron before I walked back to the door and turned the sign to open.

"Come on in." I held the door open for the woman. She stepped inside. "Can I help you with anything?"

"Just looking around." She smiled and went around the tables picking up the bottles.

"Let me know if you need anything." I inhaled when she walked by. There wasn't anything setting off my intuition of a cure she needed.

More than half of the time, the customers who walked through the door really didn't need a real cure. They were there for curiosity of what a cure shop was all about.

This was a perfect time to work on my Oscar potion.

I walked back to the shelf where I kept all the ingredients I use for my special cures. Tapping each one, I read their names out loud, trying to tap into my intuition. "Belladonna, Ferrum Phos, Sepia, Natrum Mur, Valerian Root."

My finger warmed when I touched the Eye of Saber Cat, which was my intuition telling me to pick that ingredient.

"You've never failed me yet," I said, referring to my spiritual gift of intuition. Gingerly, I picked up the container with the eyes and carefully unscrewed the lid.

Rarely did my intuition tell me to use the Eye of Saber Cat and it freaked me out every time I opened the jar because all the eyes looked at me.

"Okay," I sighed and opened the jar. All the eyes shifted right and left when the light entered. "Which one of you is going to bring Oscar back to me?"

I took the tongs and haphazardly grabbed one not looking into the eye. I dropped it into the cauldron.

After that I grabbed a few extra ingredients—for good measure. The customers that were standing in line at Glorybee filed in one by one.

"Welcome," I said, poking my head out from behind the partition. "I'll be with you in a minute." The bell over the door dinged a few more times.

Quickly I stirred the potion. I grabbed the purple heart bottle with the potion I had started earlier. I unscrewed the top and put a few sprinkles of it into the cauldron.

The Eye of Saber Cat seemed to be doing the trick with the swirling chunky liquid rising to the top with a cerulean glow. A dash of Kali phos would make the liquid stop rising and take a little edge off of Oscar's nervous system with the positive benefits of opening up to love—my love.

"There is my favorite little witch." The voice rounded the corner of the partition.

Oscar appeared with Mr. Prince Charming in his arms. They had a newfound friendship. Mr. Prince Charming had always been a tad-bit, a whole hell of a lot, jealous of my feelings for Oscar, but since Oscar lost his spiritual memory, Mr. Prince Charming thought he was the cat's meow.

"Look who I found sitting on the steps." He put Mr. Prince Charming on the counter.

"My two favorite men," I joked and dusted my hands off on my apron. I took Oscar by the arm to lead him away from the cauldron, which he didn't need to see or ask about. He rubbernecked trying to get a glimpse of what I was doing. I rubbernecked to get a glimpse of his hot bottom in the Locust Grove police uniform. "I'm not a witch," I whispered dragging him around the counter. "And you don't work here so you have to stay on that side of the line." My foot dragged on the floor to make an invisible line.

"Oh, I think you are a witch." He winked. "Maybe we should call you Samantha from Bewitched. Did she have a cat?"

"I don't know?" I rubbed Mr. Prince Charming's ears. "Stop calling me a witch. What are you doing here?" Not that I minded. Two times in one day and I was not complaining. Plus it wasn't even lunch time either.

My toes curled. There was no way he was passing through Whispering Falls for work. He had to have come here to see me.

"I came to see Arabella." There was a smile in his voice, something that wasn't sitting well with my heart. He stood with his hands clasped in front of him. That damn uniform made him look mighty fine. For a second I thought I would shove the unfinished potion down his throat and scream, *fall in love with me!*

"You did?" I played stupid.

He leaned in and bumped me in a playful way. He looked at me for a long moment, as though he was trying to find the right words or assess what I was thinking. He'd blush if he knew what I was thinking.

"You aren't a tad bit jealous are you, June Heal?" His lips were so close, I had to force myself not to cling to them like a magnet. I didn't move. It was like I was hypnotized. He lifted a hand and rubbed it down my check. "Oh June."

He threw his head back. His blue eyes danced with amusement.

Meow, meow. Mr. Prince Charming jumped off the counter and darted around my ankles, causing me to step back. He wasn't happy with the closeness but I was. I pushed him aside with my foot. He wasn't pleased. He jumped back up on the counter, threw his leg in the air and started to clean himself.

"Stop it!" I shooed him off and glared at him. That whole cat grooming thing was nasty and I didn't want it on the counter of the store and he knew it.

Rowl! Mr. Prince Charming showed his teeth and ran out the cat door.

"That was interesting." Oscar had moved away, taking his smell with him. I sniffed a little harder to try to soak in all that I could before he left.

"You drove all this way to see someone you don't know?" I had to get back on topic.

"Arabella wanted some information about security. I told her I could install a system for her. She said that sounded great and we could talk about it over lunch at The Gathering Grove." He looked at his wrist watch. "I'll get to see you for dinner." His brows rose.

I snapped my fingers. "Oh, I forgot I have a meeting tonight so I won't be able to make it for dinner."

"Oh." He gave me a smile that didn't quite make it to his eyes. "That's fine. I guess a witch has got to do what a witch has got to do," he joked.

"Not funny." I held up a finger for him to hold on while I went behind the counter and grabbed a mojo bag filled with dream sprinkles. I slipped it into the pocket of my jeans so he didn't see. "I'm actually hungry, so I can go to lunch with you."

"You have a shop full of customers." He made a good point. "Pretty. Arabella's work?" He poked at the flowers.

"Oh, I forgot to thank you for them." I hooked my arm into Oscar's. My whole being seemed to be filled with joy when I was with him.

"You are welcome." His gaze sent chills all over my body. "But I didn't send any flowers."

"Really?" My entire romantic idea of him dropping to one knee had just flown out the window.

"June has a secret admirer," Oscar teased.

I bit my lip. There were no secrets around Whispering Falls. Now I had to find out who sent me wildflowers. Pretty ones too.

"Come join us if you can. And I'm taking a rain check for dinner." Oscar walked out. The bell of the door dinged. My breath caught. My stomach dropped.

"Can I get this in a bigger size?" A customer pushed a bottle in my face.

"Hold on one sec," I pushed it out of my way and walked over to the window. I parted the curtains to get a better view of the street.

Arabella had already hooked her arm on Oscar's elbow. The image of her tall, thin body and swinging long hair next to my hunky dark-haired Oscar in his uniform brought tears to my eyes.

"I'm sorry. I'm in a hurry." The customer stood next to me holding the bottle in the air. "Are you going to help me or not?"

Chapter Nine

With a hop and a skip, I mixed up a few remaining potions for the other customers in the store. Nothing that required a lot of time which was exactly what I needed. I had to get over to The Gathering Grove Tea Shoppe to see what Arabella had up her magical little sleeve. Plus I wanted to ask her about the flowers. If Oscar hadn't sent them, who had? I grabbed a protection mojo bag to give Oscar. He was in definite need for protection against Arabella and her good-smelling flowers.

"Off and running again?" Chandra stood outside of A Cleansing Spirit Spa with Petunia, Clyde perched on her shoulder. She had Petunia's hand firmly grasped in hers; getting a good look at the ring Gerald had given Petunia.

There was no time for chit-chat or gawking of the ring. I pulled the shop door closer to me and jiggled the handle after I locked the door.

"You have been on the run all morning long and it's just after noon." Petunia had clearly noticed my comings and goings of the morning.

Don't get sucked into their conversation, I repeated to myself. It was so easy and not out of the norm to drop everything to find time for idle chit-chat in Whispering Falls.

"I was just telling Chandra how lovely the orchids were that you had sent over," Petunia said, totally sucking me in.

I skipped down the front step and out of the gate toward them. "I'm not sure what you are talking about."

"The beautiful orchid arrangement." Her lips twitched into a nervous smile. Her brows frowned.

She reached up and stroked Clyde. The diamond caught my eye. It was the same diamond I had picked out for Oscar to give me when he proposed. My mouth dropped. *Arabella.*

"You know. I pointed to them this morning while I was grooming Clyde." She said in dazed exasperation.

"About that, I didn't send you any flowers." I put my hand out to touch her arm for a little comfort. Oddly, she slinked away. "As a matter of fact, someone sent me flowers too."

"But the card stated they were from you, June Heal." A sudden thin chill hung in her words. The tension could have been cut with Clyde's talons.

"Well, they weren't. I'll see what the mix up is when I talk to Arabella." I pointed over to The Gathering Grove where she and Oscar were at one of those café tables on the sidewalk.

"We did notice the two of them having lunch." Chandra used her chubby fingers to push her turban a little further up on her forehead as if she wasn't getting a good enough look with her gawking stare.

"Business. They are discussing security and stuff." I smiled trying to hide my intuition that told me I should be fearful. The best way to not be fearful would be to ignore the gut feeling because I wasn't sure if it was my emotions guiding the fear or if it was something I really did need to listen to. "Not that she doesn't flirt with every guy she sees," I muttered.

"Now you're talking!" Chandra smacked her hands and rubbed them together so fast, I was sure there would be smoke coming from them soon. "I knew there was something with you today."

"What? Nothing." I put my hand in the air. "I swear."

Lied again.

"Um hmmm. We'll see," Petunia added fuel to the fire when I walked away.

Arabella was leaving as I walked up.

"All yours for now." She winked, tossing her long hair behind her.

"Hello you two." Gerald rushed over with his pad of paper and pen in hand. He curled the edge of his mustache with one hand and lowered his eyes. "Might I get you a spot of noon tea, June?"

"That'd be great. Oscar?" I scooted the chair closer to the table. I noticed he only had a glass of water.

"Yea, sounds great." He didn't look up at me. He was too busy checking his cell phone.

Gerald hurried off, his fancy coattails flying behind him. He always was dressed so dapper, unlike his lady love and that bird's nest hair-do of hers. My eyes slid over to A Cleansing Spirit Spa. Chandra and Petunia were both still staring.

Before Oscar and I could start a conversation Gerald was back with a tray filled with a tea pot and a tea cup with a saucer. The old smooth white Dalton tea cup looked awfully familiar. Silently Oscar and I watched Gerald begin his magic journey of pouring tea.

"This is an art form you know," Gerald ground the leaves in a bowl using a mortar-and-pestle-type tool and then brushed powder into the tea pot where he let it steep it for a few seconds. The tea cup was never at eye level which made me even more suspicious. "The leaves have to be just perfect."

Just perfect? Perfect for what? I eyed him warily.

Gerald put the Dalton cup on the table and held the pot high in the air dipping it forward letting all the hot steamed water pour directly into the cup. The bobbling leaf caught my attention.

Beep, beep. Oscar looked down and fiddled with his cell.

"Oops. Duty calls." He jumped up. "I'll call you to make new plans. Sorry."

"But wait!" Gerald protested. "Just take a sip and tell me how you like it."

"Ehehehenngh." I pushed the cup and saucer away knowing exactly what Gerald had up his sleeves. His magical tea-reading sleeves. But why would he want to read Oscar?

Oscar didn't wait around anyway. He was in his car with the lights and sirens blaring.

"What was that about?" Gerald plopped down in Oscar's chair.

"You tell me." Did he really think he was going to pull a fast one over on me?

"What?" Gerald shrugged giving a little smirk. "He's not a spiritualist. I can read him in my own shop."

"He was a spiritualist and I'm trying to get him in that place again." I patted the mojo bag buried deep in my pocket. My idea of slipping him some sweet dream mix and putting a little of me in his dream was also going to have to wait.

"Are you okay, June?" Gerald was always good at reading me without the leaves.

"Not really. Don't get me wrong. I'm happy for you and Petunia, but I really thought the headline was going to be about me and Oscar." I picked up the tea and started to drink it forgetting about the leaves. "Mmm. This is really good." I tossed back the rest of it and set the cup on the table.

Gerald looked down at the cup. His mouth dropped. Sheer fright settled in his little beady eyes.

"Gerald, are *you* okay?" Suddenly the question seemed to fit him more than me.

Slowly he shook his head. He held his finger in the air. It trembled. He pulled it back and balled his hand into a tight fist. "The…the…the cup," his voice quivered.

I peered into it. The leaves were scattered all around the edges.

"Oh no." My head dropped. Gerald had seen something.

"The headlines." Gerald went into a fog like I had seen him do so many times before when he was reading someone's leaves. "You have to break a few eggs before you make an omelet."

"Does that have to do with me?" I knew better than to ask. Run, my mind told me. But I couldn't. I sat there like my butt was cemented to the chair.

"Yes." The fear had left his eyes and dripped all over his face. "They are evil. They will bring death."

"Who? Who is going to bring death?" I asked.

Gerald looked out the window. He was looking into the future. I waved my hand in front of him, but he was not there.

Chapter Ten

I looked down at Mr. Prince Charming as we were
making our way back to the shop. "What were Gerald and
Arabella talking about earlier?" I asked Mr.
Prince Charming, who appeared out of nowhere and like he was
going to open his little mouth and tell me the big secret.
"Do you think he picked up on my vibes about Arabella?
How does he know her?" I continued to ask my fairy-god
cat questions I knew he couldn't answer, but it put deep
suspicion in my mind.

As I recalled, Gerald and Arabella didn't seem to be
having a pleasant conversation. Definitely something to
look into. Gerald said the evil was coming into my life.
Was Arabella a coincidence? I thought not.

I wasn't going to lie. The way Gerald reacted did give
me pause which sort of made me want to run to my cottage
where I could pull the covers over my head and not come
out until the wedding was over, because somehow I felt all
of this was tied to their day of wedded bliss. Really I didn't
need Gerald's reaction as an excuse. I just wanted their
wedding to be over and all the hubbub to go away.

"June!" Petunia waved her hand in the air from the
front steps of Glorybee Pet Shop. An instrumental mix of
all sorts of animals played like a symphony through the
opened shop door. Petunia had it propped open with her
foot. "I want to have my shower pretty soon because I'm
going to tell Gerald I want to get married ASAP!"

"As in less than a week?" Stunned, I stopped dead in
my tracks. Things were getting stranger and stranger as the
day went on.

"Yes. As in a few days." She greeted a couple of
customers coming into her shop. "We will talk at the

meeting! Oh, and I need a few spiders. Alive. One more thing."

Spiders? Alive? Instantly I knew the jar of spiders KJ had left were for Petunia. I wondered what she needed with them. Mr. Prince Charming ran in front of me with his long white tail swaying in the afternoon sun.

"What is it?" I grinded my teeth together with the fake smile planted across my face.

"Arabella said she'd handle all the flowers and a wedding in a couple of days is no problem for her."

"Of course she said that." I glared and turned my attention toward Mr. Prince Charming.

He was on the top step swatting a few cicadas and eating them whole.

"What is wrong with you?" My face curled. The thought of eating a nasty insect was too much to bear. "Are you hungry?" I asked Mr. Prince Charming.

Mewwwl. His response was long and drawn out. His normal "I'm starving, feed me" response.

He darted into the shop when I opened the door, rushing back to the storage room door where I kept a small refrigerator and a small couch for those late nights. His bowl was there along with a few play toys. He never played. I don't know what I was thinking when I had bought all the toys. He was a fairy-god cat...not a real cat.

"I'll be with you in just a second," I said to the customer coming in the shop behind me. "Got to feed the cat." I gestured toward Mr. Prince Charming who was already scratching up the storage room door as if he was about to eat the wood scrapings his long claws carved out of the door.

The customer happily moved around the shop picking up different bottles and reading the labels which was what most customers did. There wasn't a vibe nor did my intuition tell me the customer needed a special potion. All was good in A Charming Cure with the exception of a staring Mr. Prince Charming.

"What is your problem?" I asked the ornery cat. This was very unusual behavior from him. He darted to the small refrigerator where I made extra food for him. Since I was a homeopathic spiritualist I made his food and portioned it out according to what he was supposed to have. He wasn't supposed to be eating in the afternoon. "You must be going through a growing spurt," I joked.

No one really knew Mr. Prince Charming's age. The only thing I knew for sure was that he came when I was ten, which meant I had had him for eighteen years and he hadn't aged a day.

I put a little extra scoop in his bowl and before I could put the container away, he had eaten all of it and wanted more.

"No." My eyes narrowed. "You can't possibly be hungry."

Did Mr. Prince Charming have something wrong with him?

I worried there was an underlying medical condition. Even though I had never taken him to the veterinarian before, maybe I should. Or I could take him to Petunia. I bet she would be able to tell me what was wrong.

"Looks like we need to call Richard Simmons," Madame Torres lit up. A picture of the workout icon appeared in her glass ball. I grabbed her and shoved her underneath the counter, away from the customer's ears. She did have a way with words. A way that grated on anyone's nerves.

Rowl! Mr. Prince Charming shrieked and ran out of the storage room before I could grab him up and rush him over to Petunia.

"I will catch you!" I screamed after him. The customer looked up with wide eyes and watched Mr. Prince Charming. "Is there something I can help you with?" I kindly asked the customer one more time so as not to alarm her of the strange cat behavior. Mr. Prince Charming knew good and well if she wasn't there I'd have ran out after him to nail down exactly why he was eating so much.

The customer shook her head and went on about her business as I looked out the window at Mr. Prince Charming darting into town making note of his erratic movements.

I grabbed my phone out of my back pocket and quickly dialed Oscar. If anyone knew what to do with a cat, a cat that had something wrong, he would.

"Hey, June." That deep, dripping with hunky voice answered the phone causing my knees to buckle and my heart to skip a beat…or two.

"I'm sorry to bother you," truly I wasn't, "but Mr. Prince Charming seems to be acting funny."

"Well he is a funny…er …different cat." He laughed probably trying to throw me off of what he had said because normally I would die at the fact he would call Mr. Prince Charming a funny or strange cat.

"No, I mean funny as in sick."

"Is he throwing up hairballs? Or eating grass?" He spouted out the normal signs of a sick animal.

"No. He is eating all the time." There were a million different diseases that went through my head and each one scared me to death.

"That's what cats do. Eat mice, eat bunnies…"

"No," I whispered into the phone. "He doesn't eat any of those things."

The thought of Mr. Prince Charming bringing home a dead mouse or cute little bunny was something I didn't want to picture nor see.

"He's scratching the door and leaving marks." I glanced back at the door where Mr. Prince Charming had gone nuts ripping it to shreds and noticed the scratches made a perfect circle, like a wedding ring. "Oh my God!" I gasped and dropped the phone.

Mr. Prince Charming wasn't hungry, he was trying to tell me something. I grabbed my phone off the ground, my bag with Madame Torres in it, and the jar of spiders.

"I'll call you back," I told Oscar before I ushered the customer out the door, then closed and locked it. I had a fairy-god cat to find.

The only place I knew to look first would be the pet store. He loved to go over there and visit with his other animal friends. I had never seen anything like Glorybee Pet Shop. Petunia had every single kind of animal and rodent living under the same roof in harmony, throwing the food chain right out the window. Mr. Prince Charming had a fond affection for one of the squirrels.

Glorybee was at the far end of Main Street, a couple of doors down from A Charming Cure and next to A Cleansing Spirit Spa.

I glanced in the spa and Chandra was hunkered over some woman's hand rubbing lotion all over it and her mouth was running a mile a minute. Little did the woman realize Chandra was a palm reader and being a manicurist was her cover. Women from all over loved to come get their nails done by Chandra. She would tell them things that were going to happen in their future or give them unsolicited advice, with them never knowing she was reading their palm.

Once some of the advice came true for them, they would come back for more. That was the best part of Whispering Falls. All the visitors felt the magic, only they couldn't put their fingers on it, making them come back over and over again.

The instant smell of animals hit me when I pushed the heavy electric-blue wood door open to the pet shop. It had wavy yellow metal detailing that resembled the branches of a tree.

There wasn't anything normal about Glorybee. I wasn't sure, but I swear I saw a hedgehog run and then roll across the grassy floor over to the real life tree that stood in the corner of the room. A bird skimmed the top of my head and landed on a branch next to a grey squirrel.

Petunia Shrubwood was standing near the full grown maple. Her hand was flailing in the air going down the line of people looking at her ring. *My ring.*

The squirrel jumped from the lower branch and onto Petunia's shoulder. He too was getting a good look at the shiner.

"Petunia Regiula," she said her new name, pride dripping all over her face. There wasn't any hesitation in her voice. "Petunia Regiula."

She glanced over at me and waved.

I held the jar in the air and waved it around so it would make her rush over and I didn't have to fight the crowd or continue to hear all the details of her new happiness that secretly made me nauseous.

"Thank you so much June." Petunia grabbed the jar and held it up to the light. The spiders stayed at the top of the cheese cloth lid desperately trying to get out.

The lady who had gotten her daughter the fancy fertility potion was in the back of Glorybee looking at the

firefly kits. She smiled and drummed her fingers in the air
while mouthing hello.

My soul grinned. I could picture her daughter and
grandchild playing in a back yard full of fireflies.
Especially ones that never died.

The firefly kits Petunia sells were special. Fireflies
were the teenagers that have passed, like most of the
animals in Glorybee. When a spiritual soul passed to the
afterlife, some could come back in the form of animals and
the fireflies were always teenagers.

It was a perfect fit for them. Teenagers sleep all day,
like fireflies and fireflies are up all night, just like
teenagers. And the afterlife animals stayed alive making
good on the earth and with the people they love.

Little did the woman know that if she did purchase the
kit, she would be blessed with fireflies all year around.
There really was nothing more beautiful than a starry black
night with the light of the tiny creatures—and any child
would love that. The warm glow of being able to help
someone made me feel good inside.

"Do you know her?" Petunia asked.

"She is a customer." I turned my attention to my happy
friend. Even though I was a little envious, I was happy for
her. "You said you wanted spiders, I brought you spiders."

"Thank you." She kissed the jar before she hugged it to
her chest. "Best present ever." She grabbed me and hugged
me. "Did you see my ring?" She thrust her left hand up to
my face.

"Yes. Earlier." I smiled and looked again. I took a step
back so her hand wasn't blurred and it could come into
focus.

"I know you did. But I still can't believe it!" Petunia
gushed. "You won't believe the flowers Arabella
suggested. Not only is she beautiful, she's smart."

"Beautiful and smart." *Meh.* I barely took a glance at the ring before I started with my questions. "Have you seen Mr. Prince Charming?"

"Is that silly cat missing again?" she asked. It wasn't unusual for him to run off and come over to hang out in the tree. It was a cool tree. If I worked at Glorybee, I'd probably hang a swing from a branch and swing all day.

"He has been doing some strange things like eating a lot."

Petunia's eyes grew big. "What exactly do you mean?" She took me by the elbow and walked me to the back of the store out of the way of the customers. "I need every detail."

"So he hasn't been here and you know?" I waved my hand around her head. She knew I was asking if she had somehow used her spiritual gift to talk to him.

"No. He hasn't." She shook her head. A few dried leaves fell out and tumbled to the ground. She looked down. "Oh dear."

For the first time since the big proposal, Petunia didn't have a happy bride-to-be smile planted across her face.

"What?" I asked and watched her pick up the crispy brown leaves.

"This is not good, June Heal." She pushed her hands in her hair making more dried leaves, brown berries—that I was sure were supposed to be a color—and some brittle sticks fall out the other side. "Things are dying."

"Dying?"

She held the jar up to the light. Sure enough, the spiders in the jar were no longer crawling all over the cheese cloth lid. They were lying dead at the bottom.

Chapter Eleven

"This is not good, this is not good." Petunia marched around her shop, ushering all of the customers out the door. "I'm closed for the rest of the day," she told them and pushed them out.

"Trouble in paradise," Madame Torres chirped from deep within my bag. "History will always catch up to you." There was a little too much pleasure in her voice. I tucked my bag up under my arm so Petunia wouldn't hear her and get even more freaked out.

"Petunia, what about Mr. Prince Charming?" I asked.

"Not good." She shook her head and more dried things that I couldn't even tell what they were fell out and to the ground in piles as she walked. "None of this is good. You go and get ready for the meeting and be sure to bring materials for an impromptu smudging ceremony." She barked orders at me as she took scoops of food and put them in bowls all over the shop.

"Are you feeling okay?" I asked her. The color in her face had turned ashen.

She ran around the shop putting things on not only the wrong shelves, but in the wrong aisles as well. Her normal routine before closing was brushing the animals, bathing if needed, and pretty much hand feeding them before she even thought about going to the back of the shop to her apartment. Not today. She was worried.

"Go!" Her eyes were wide open and she flung her hands in the air. "What are you waiting for?"

"I sort of wanted to know what is not good and what is wrong with Mr. Prince Charming." The answers I had come to seek weren't answered. "Is all of this tied together?"

Petunia stopped. Her grey face now had a frightened tight jaw. The lines between her eyes creased when she furrowed her brows.

"Please tell me," I begged to know. Even though I was the Village President, I didn't know everything about the spiritual world or what the spiritualist was capable of. They had lived here all their lives and I had only been here a year and only President for a few short months so I couldn't possibly know every single detail of the spiritual life. Only what I was living.

"I'm relying on all of you to tell me what is going on." I ran my hands down her arm.

"I can't be so sure I can trust you." She stood stoic, not moving. Her stone cold eyes sent chills up my spine.

"Do you think I'm the enemy?" I questioned her. "I'm here to help."

"If you are here to help and you are my friend," she drew in a deep breath, "you would be happy for me. But you haven't been. And all of these things, dead spiders, dried leaves, and a hungry cat are all bad omens for an upcoming wedding."

"Oh," I laughed. "You can't possibly believe in superstition?" That was the silliest thing I had heard. "We are Good-Sider spiritualists. We wave off the bad juju."

Gently I reminded her about the two spiritual sides. There are Good-Sider and Dark-Sider spiritualists. Good-Siders only seek the good in the spiritual world and see the good in the customers seeking guidance. Which meant there was no way I was going to deliver bad news to anyone seeking a cure that came into my store. There was always a positive side to everything. Plus we held the secret to the *Ultimate Spell*. A secret spell that would allow the Dark-Siders to take over.

Not all Dark-Siders are bad. And when I took over as Village President, I didn't like the fact Whispering Falls was only a Good-Sider village. I changed the law, allowing all spiritualists to come, live, and own a shop. The only Dark-Siders in our village were Eloise and Raven, both very nice and neither had a bad bone in their body. But Arabella? There was little I knew about her. Was that her problem? Was she the one stirring the pot in all of this mess?

"That is the one thing I can't stand about you June Heal!" Petunia opened the heavy front door and held it for me. "You should have never been appointed Village President. You know nothing about the spiritual world. Everything is not always fixed with a little potion. I thought you'd figured that out by now since you can't seem to make Oscar Park fall back in love with you."

"Now who is jealous?" Madame Torres's light was glowing from the bag.

"Petunia," I had never heard such ugly things come out of her mouth. "Leave Oscar out of this. This is about you and why you think the world is about to come to an end."

"It is! It's my world that is coming to an end." Petunia pushed me out the door. I looked at her.

"How do dead leaves symbolize your life coming to an end? Or Mr. Prince Charming becoming a fatty in his old age?" I tried to make light of the situation as much as possible. This was not what I had intended to happen when I had gone over there. Besides, this was what I did. I made everyone feel better during a time of crisis while I figured out how to end the crisis so no one's life would be interrupted.

"Because she is old." Madame Torres was having too much fun at the expense of Petunia's issues.

"June." Petunia planted her hands on her hips. "These are all signs of death of an engagement. I'm the only one engaged."

Instantly I felt so happy that I wasn't.

"We can forget all of that. I'm going to have your shower and show you how everyone is happy for you and supports you." I gulped. "I will do a special smudge tonight before the Village meeting."

"You will?" There was a little relief in her voice.

"Yes," I confirmed.

"Still." She dropped her hands to her side. "I have to tell Gerald about all of the signs."

"Okay." I smiled knowing it was not good that she see Gerald.

After all, Gerald was walking toward us like a zombie.

"Gerald, Gerald?" Petunia waved her hand in front of him when he walked past her. His hat was not on top of his head, which I believed only happened when he slept. He was never without the hat. And his mustache was protruding in all different directions. He certainly wasn't the dapper fellow we were used to seeing. "Are you okay?"

Hrmph. Gerald cleared his throat before he came to an abrupt stop. "I…" He turned around. An element of fear showed on his face. "I..," he paused, "I was just coming to see my lovely bride-to-be."

When he took her into his arms, he looked at me over her shoulders. His brows lowered and he pursed his lips into a silent *shhh* and slowly shook his head.

"Gerald," Petunia pulled away and slightly turned to me. "Don't you think it would be a good idea to get married as soon as possible?"

"She's scared of losing him," Madame Torres said from the bottom of the bag. I tried to muffle her as she talked because Gerald had a better trained ear than Petunia and I didn't want him to know she was giving her crystal ball opinion.

Petunia turned around, there was a deep worry set in her eyes. I didn't know if she was responding to what Madame Torres had said.

All these weird signs were coming to light. Flowers were being delivered, which had to do with Arabella. Arabella was taking secretively to Gerald and making the moves on Oscar. I knew that Petunia had dried leaves and crap falling out of her hair, which happened when things die—they shrivel up. The spiders were now curled up in a tiny balls dead at the bottom of the jar. And I knew that Mr. Prince Charming needed to see a veterinarian because he was going to eat me out of house and home before he started on the cicada population. Who knew what was next on his menu.

"I think we should let June have your bridal shower and keep things as planned." He looked at me and so did Petunia. "Don't you, June?"

Petunia's eyes grew big like she was saying *oh no you better not agree with him.*

"You two leave me out of it." I put my hands in front of me. I still had to find my cat and this was not something to get in the middle of. I had my own problems. "You two are the ones who are getting married. I'm just the host of the party."

"Arabella is already getting the flowers together," Petunia told him. "We need to have it ASAP. Why wait?"

I walked between them and stopped.

"When you decide, let me know. But I'm going to go on with my plans of having your shower in a couple of days."

I walked off without giving them another opportunity to have me referee the argument between the two of them when neither of them had given good reasons to support their side. It was all a bit confusing to me. The ever-so-happy, newly-engaged couple stood on Main Street fighting where they had only stood hours ago getting engaged.

Chapter Twelve

Petunia was able to read animals, not predict the future. The dying spiders, the twigs in her hair, and the color draining from her face were sure signs that something was going on.

I left her and Gerald to work out their differences on when the wedding was going to take place, but not before she made me promise to have the shower tomorrow.

Tomorrow.

The grey sky fit my mood, leaving me less than motivated to bring all things—something old, something new, something borrowed, and something blue—together in less than twenty-four hours.

"Trouble in paradise," Madame Torres said the words I was thinking from the depth of my bag. I snuggled her close to me in case someone heard her. The best thing for me was to stay low-key until the wedding was over. Whether it was in a day or in a couple of weeks, I could keep it together with a big smile on my face.

"Yes." I jiggled my keys in the door of A Charming Cure and looked back before we went in. "I'm not sure why there is trouble, but a good smudging ceremony just might do the trick."

Mr. Prince Charming darted in, almost knocking me on my butt as my feet got tangled up.

I caught the edge of one of the tables to steady myself. The base of the light rattled, almost falling over. I quickly grabbed it so it wouldn't tumble and crash my potion bottles to the ground.

"That was a close one." I glared at Mr. Prince Charming who had taken his rightful spot on the counter with his leg in the air as he cleaned himself. Not a care in the world.

There were times when he was a plain old cat and then there were times he seemed to really get what was going on in the spiritual world. Today he seemed like the old stray cat that wandered into my life many moons ago.

He didn't seem to notice the disapproving look I gave him for his odd behavior. Or he didn't care.

"Thanks for almost killing me," I quipped in his direction when I walked behind the counter to get ready for the smudging ceremony.

Meow. Mr. Prince Charming did his round-about moves and finally settled in a ball next to the cash register.

The light rap at the door caught my attention.

Ophelia waved when I looked toward the door.

"Hey," I greeted her when I opened the door. I held it open. "Come on in. I'm just about to get the smudge together for the meeting."

"Oh." Ophelia stepped inside and brushed her honey-colored curls behind her shoulder before she unbuttoned her red, full-length coat. "It's chilly out there."

I glanced out. The grey sky had taken over the entire village and hung low, almost low enough to touch. The chill rushed in after Ophelia, zipping to my bones. I shivered.

"Get in." I rushed her inside and shut the door behind her.

"Did you say you were going to be doing a smudging ceremony?" she asked and placed her coat on the door knob before she followed me back to the shop.

"There are some strange things going on around here and a cleansing smudge isn't going to hurt." The shelf of ingredients was nice and full from KJ's visit.

There were so many options to choose from. The dry salt was the first ingredient that touched my intuition when I looked at it.

"I know!" She gasped. "Like the weather." She droned on about how she and Colton were eating a muffin from Wicked Good on Colton's break. They watched the grey sky roll in like a tidal wave. "Plus I saw the little spat between the love birds."

I turned toward Ophelia. Her face was clouded with uneasiness.

"You too?" I could see it. She had worry written all over her.

Ophelia shifted, she bit her lip on the corner.

"Oh come on." I assured her and turned back to my ingredient shelf. I pulled down the dry salt bottle and set it next to the cauldron. Dry salt was used to drive away negative energy and the way Ophelia and Petunia were acting, there was negative energy in those dark clouds. I was going to brush those away. "Nothing is going on. We are just having some sort of change in the weather pattern." I gulped, trying to believe in what I was saying. "You know all that talk about the ozone layers depleting and all that stuff." I waved my hand in the air before grabbing a couple of stalks of sage.

"It just seems a little odd." She rapped her fingers on the counter. "Don't you think?"

"I think everyone is creating all this bad energy." I reached back on the shelf and grabbed some Argentum Nitricum, good for fear and nervousness. It would be a good little additive for the smudge. Oh! The sweet grass caught my eye. It was a wonderful herb to encourage kindness.

"Colton is ready for anything. He even called back to the village in Ohio to see if they were having the same weather." Ophelia and Colton came from a village in Ohio.

"Speaking of Colton," I had to change the subject, "did you tell him about the sleeping aide?"

The lavender stalks would be another great ingredient for the village. I plucked a few stalks from the lavender bundle and tied it to the sage before I sprinkled some dry salt and Argentums Nitricum on it.

"No," Ophelia stressed. "I thought I would just slip it into his chamomile tea tonight."

I laughed. She was a sneaky one. Then my gut tangled with my intuition. There was a sudden fear and the game of "what if". What if something bad happened and we needed our sheriff?

Slowly I eased back to the ingredients so I wouldn't alarm Ophelia and grabbed a couple stalks of juniper to add to the bundle. Juniper was a great herb to use because it will help us help ourselves and with everyone going a little coo-coo, it wasn't going to hurt to cover all the bases.

"Let me know how it works. We don't want him to be flat out cold. We want him to just sleep deeply enough not to snore." I picked up dry salt and added a few more dashes, just for precaution.

"Are you ready?" I asked and grabbed my box of matches that were stored under the counter along with my feather from Clyde, Petunia's bird. It was a long full, thick tail feather that was perfect to sweep the smudge smoke into the crowd so they could receive the full effect of the powers of the ceremony.

"I am." She grabbed her coat and swung it around her shoulders. She quickly buttoned it up. "You probably need to grab your coat."

"Good thinking." I went to the back of the shop and grabbed it before we left.

On our way around the shop and up the hill, I decided to use the time to ask her about Arabella.

"Have you gone by Magical Moments?" That was my way of getting some gossip from her.

"I did." Ophelia was tight lipped.

"And?" This was proving to be harder than I thought. Ophelia Biblio was fairly new to the community and I wasn't sure how much she did gossip, but what young girl didn't? I needed someone on my side and it might as well be her.

"She has some great style." There was a spark in her eye. So...young women like style and Arabella had plenty of that. "She has some great ideas for Petunia's shower."

There was no sense in trying to dig for more dirt on Arabella. She might not be all evil, but she wasn't pulling the wool over my eyes. Someone sent those flowers and it wasn't me.

"Like what?" Haphazardly I asked, bringing the bundle closer to my body as the night air whipped around.

"She said she has some really cool edible flowers that will float in a punch bowl that she's making. And..." Ophelia went on and on about Arabella and her *great* ideas. Her voice drifted as my eyes caught sight of the Gathering Rock.

The dusk light was much darker than normal. It looked like someone had started a fire in the middle of the gathering space.

The Gathering Rock was where we held all of our village meetings. It was a safe and sacred place for all spiritualists to gather. The focal point was a big rock that stood at the front of the gathering space, which was a wide open space for us to have chairs, benches, or stand if we wanted to.

Most meetings weren't attended by all, but tonight there seemed to be a crowd. Their voices immediately dampened to a hushed whisper when they saw me and Ophelia walk up.

"Good evening." I looked everyone in the eye as I approached and smiled.

There was a desolate feeling lingering around the space, making it difficult for my head to clear for the ceremony. Everyone was feeling the heavy blanket that had covered Whispering Falls.

The council, which included Izzy, Gerald, Petunia, and Chandra, was already seated at the front of the Gathering Rock.

I was particularly interested in Gerald and Petunia. Petunia had her back to Gerald who was begging her to look at him. Leaves were falling out of her hair by the second.

"Good evening." I laid the bundle on the table and grabbed the gavel so I could hit it on the rock and bring the meeting to order.

"You are going to talk about the unfortunate weather we are having, right?" Izzy asked.

In other words she was telling me to make sure I was positive and didn't alarm anyone.

"Of course I am." I turned and banged the gavel on the rock. The crowd took a seat. Even the ones who normally stood the entire meeting took a seat on the ground or found a vacant chair. "The monthly village meeting of the Whispering Falls community is now coming to order!" I shouted and banged the rock several times.

The echo of the gavel bit the silence of the air. I hit it another time for good measure...or stalling for time.

"Good evening." I laid the gavel back on the table. "As you can see we are having some sort of weather pattern coming through the valley and settling in a bit." I turned and picked up the smudge and feather.

"Weather pattern?" someone from the crowd asked in a sarcastic tone.

I swallowed, trying to ignore them, but who was I trying to kid? I was amongst a group of spiritualists who knew something wasn't right. Try as I might, it was still my duty to keep everyone calm and at peace so we could continue to have a solid village.

"I'd like to start the meeting off by doing a little cleansing smudge." I chose to ignore the heckler and light the bundle. Slowly I walked up and down the space, swerving in and out of the spiritualists with the smoldering herbs while fanning the smoke with the feather.

I chanted a few words of encouragement. Nothing special. Just something that came to my mind as I walked around smelling the fumes and trying to cleanse the earth. Arabella sat in the back corner on the ground with her eyes closed.

I turned the bundle to where I had put the sweet grass. If anyone needed to be kinder and have a better attitude, it was her.

Cough, cough. Arabella glanced up at me. Her eyes were barely visible through all the smoke I had swept over her and around her. There was enough smoke around her to look like she was smoking a pipe.

"I never," she gasped and stood up. "I never have seen someone screw up a smudging ceremony."

There was an audible gasp over the crowd. Everyone's mouth was open and all their eyes were on Arabella Paxton, though we could only see the whites of her socks, as she stomped back down the hill.

With a little check in the score box for me, I smiled and made my way back up to the front of the Gathering Rock to start the meeting.

"First I would like to congratulate Petunia Shrubwood and Gerald Regiula on their engagement." I clapped my hands together encouraging the other spiritualists to do the same. "And I would like to invite you all to an open engagement party tomorrow on Main Street."

"Engagement party?" Petunia's eyes lit up. It was the only thing not looking a little peaked on her entire person. She clasped her hands together and turned her body toward Gerald. "That's so much better than a bridal shower."

"Whatever makes you happy." Gerald nodded. The happiness was obviously not shared by the scowl on his face. "When did you say this was going to happen?"

"Tomorrow." Before the word left my mouth, a clap of thunder cracked over the village followed up by a few streaks of lightning. "And we better get this meeting started."

The sky was getting darker and scarier by the second. We made a couple of amendments to the rules, which included Rule Number Three. That was the rule where only one shop owner per couple or household. Whichever way you looked at it, it was dumb.

"All in favor say 'yea'." I smacked the gavel. The crowd roared. Just for legality's sake and to cover all the bases, I asked, "All not in favor say 'nay'."

There was silence.

"This meeting is now adjourned." I banged the gavel several times.

It didn't take long for the crowd to scatter. With the sounds in the sky, I was about to scat myself. That was before Petunia and Gerald started arguing…again.

"This is ridiculous." Petunia stomped out from behind her chair. "We have been waiting years for this."

"Exactly." Gerald threw his hands in the air. "That is what I'm saying! What is the hurry? Why don't we make sure we do this right?"

"Right?" Petunia questioned him. She looked at me.

"I'm Switzerland," I joked and put my hands in the air. There was no way I was going to get in the middle of the argument. I pretended to get all my items gathered up and not pay any attention, but I was all ears.

"And, and…," Petunia stumbled for the right words, "what do you mean by the right time? It is right. Right now!"

"But you have had no time to plan the wedding that you deserve." Gerald was trying to pull out all the cards he could, which made my gut wonder why he was doing this.

To my understanding, I had thought men didn't really care too much about the planning of the wedding. That most of that was girly details and they just showed up for pictures and the "I do's". In this case, there was something not right with Gerald working so hard on getting Petunia to delay the big event.

"What do we need?" Petunia shook her head. She looked Gerald over with a critical eye. "All of our friends are here. We have a great florist who will do whatever it is we want. The law is now on our side and we have houses to live in. You. You are the delay." She poked him in the chest. Even in the glooming night-time grey, *my ring* glistened with each jab she made.

A clump of Petunia's hair fell to the ground.

Gerald watched with sheer fright on his face. He looked at Petunia and then over to me.

Petunia looked down. Her mouth opened, and then she snapped it closed.

"I…," Gerald seemed to struggle for the words, "I'm sorry dear. We can do whatever you want."

"Hello you two." Out of nowhere Arabella appeared out of the dark shadows. Suddenly a moonbeam darted out of the black sky like a spotlight. A spotlight on her. My eyes widened. A smile curled up on the corner of her mouth.

Gerald shifted between his feet. He was a little too fidgety for me. I watched out of the corner of my eye.

"Tell him Arabella. Tell him that it's not too much to have my flowers for a wedding, say *tomorrow*." Petunia didn't even notice the glances and glares Arabella and Gerald were giving each other, but I sure did.

"Tomorrow?" Arabella's perfectly manicured brows rose. She shot Gerald a look. She crossed her arms in front of her. "Why don't we sleep on this? I'm sure you will feel better in the morning. Isn't that right, *Madame President*?" She beamed at me. The moonbeam darkened. A clap of thunder rose.

"I say we see what the weather does." I shrugged.

"I wouldn't mind seeing what Oscar would be doing." There was a glint in her eye and I darn well knew why.

"I'm out of here." There was no need for me to stay around and listen to her badger me. I had better things to do like call Oscar and get in touch with KJ.

"Toodles." Arabella drummed her fingers in the air with a big smile planted on her face.

Did she not feel the tension around us? The evil? Was it because she put it there? The question of her being a Dark-Sider nagged at me. I figured she was a Good-Sider since her grandmother was Mary Lynn.

"Toodles," I bit back, narrowing my eyes.

Petunia and Gerald didn't even seem to notice. They were halfway down the hill heading for home so they didn't even see Arabella taunt me.

"Brush it off," Madame Torres quipped when I flung my bag over my shoulder.

Brushing it off was easier said than done. I cursed Arabella the entire way home, but quickly forgot about her when I got on my comfy glow-in-the-dark bat pajamas and eased into bed.

Mewlll, meow. Mr. Prince Charming jumped on the bed and batted at my bracelet.

"I almost forgot." I peeled the covers back and planted my feet on the ground. I had limited time when I could put the call out into the night wind for KJ and I had to have some answers.

I grabbed my coat, slipped on my shoes and with Mr. Prince Charming closely behind me, we headed outside.

The brisk air wasn't a refreshing nip on my nose, it was a bleak bit that stole my breath every time I sucked in air. I licked my finger and stuck my arm way high above my head trying to figure out which way the wind was blowing. A few tries and I felt a shift when I pointed northwest of the village.

"KJ if you can hear me, please come visit me now. This is of the upmost importance to Whispering Falls." The nagging thought of the spiders he had left bothered me and I needed some answers.

Before I turned around to walk back to the house, a blast of air followed up by flurry of heat swept my hair away from my face, leaving me with a warm wisp of air.

KJ stood before me.

"Hey June." His black eyes pierced through the night. His teeth were much whiter in the dark. He laughed and pointed at my legs where you could see the bottoms of my pajamas. "Yep. Glow-in-the-dark, cool."

"Right." I looked down. "Listen, about those spiders."

"Spiders?" An inquisitive look crossed his face.

"Yea, the jar of spiders you left for me."

"I didn't leave you any spiders. Did you order spiders?" He looked up as if he was trying to recall my last order.

"No, but you left a note." I reminded him.

He shook his head. His long dark hair swung from side to side. "Nope. I didn't leave you any spiders."

"But there was a note." Panic made my heart race.

"I never leave notes either." He crossed his arms over his massive chest. The serious look on his face told me he was not joking around.

"Ok. Thanks. That is all I wanted." Shaken I slowly walked back to my house. When Mr. Prince Charming and I got back on the porch, I turned around to tell KJ goodbye, but he was already gone.

"What is going on?" I asked Mr. Prince Charming. "The flowers, the spiders, things dying." I shook my head hoping I was going to get some sleep tonight.

Chapter Thirteen

All night long I twisted and turned. I wasn't sure what disturbed me most: Petunia and Gerald fighting, Gerald being so secretive on why he didn't want to hurry up and have the wedding, the secret that was obvious between Gerald and Arabella, or the fact Arabella was trying to get her hands on Oscar or get my goat.

The more I tried to theorize it in my head, the more and more confused I had gotten.

The only person I could go to for advice that wouldn't be busy with a shop was Eloise Sandlewood. Not only would she give me sound, solid advice, she would be able to help me with my confusion.

Eloise had become my surrogate mom in the spiritual world and had been Darla's best friend when my parents lived in Whispering Falls for a brief time. Once I discovered my lineage of being a spiritualist, I found out that Eloise was also Oscar's aunt.

Since he'd lost his powers, we had slowly been telling him about his heritage and family. He was very excited to see Eloise's very cool tree house that was deep in the woods on the outskirts of town—a little bit beyond my cottage house.

The black night sky had turned into a dull grey by morning, making my intuition alarm me that it was more than just a weather pattern. There was definite evil that lingered all throughout the village.

"Get me out of here." Madame Torres chirped from deep in my bag as I made my way out the door. There was no way I could start my day without talking to Eloise first.

"What is your problem?" I pulled Madame Torres out of my bag right at the moment I saw Mr. Prince Charming's tail darting above the tall grass in front of us. It looked as though he was pouncing side to side, front to back.

"Look at that stupid cat." Madame Torres's face appeared in the globe. Her eyes narrowed when she saw Mr. Prince Charming. "Maybe he will eat something with rabies."

"That is not a nice thing to say," I warned her as we made our way to the woods. I needed advice. I needed answers to my questions that seemed to be piling up. "I need both of you."

Madame Torres and Mr. Prince Charming were always trying to see who could one-up the other in the spiritual department of keeping me safe. It was like I was a mom of two spoiled children who played the "she loves me more" game.

"Mr. Prince Charming!" I yelled over his way. His tail stopped and he darted off the other way. "Damn cat," I grumbled watching him race as fast as he could out of sight. Thank goodness Madame Torres didn't have legs to run from me. She was good enough at disappearing for days in her glass globe when she got mad at me.

"I need you to find out what is going on with Gerald. He's holding a deep secret," I told Madame Torres. If anyone could figure out what was going on, she would. The globe went dark. I put her back in my bag and continued through the thick heavy brush leading the way to Eloise's house.

Once I made it to the clearing of the woods, I could see the back of Eloise's tree house. It was early in the morning which was prime picking time for her garden where she grew the fresh herbs she used in her morning cleanse.

Eloise's spiritual job was to walk down Main Street in the early morning before the crow crowed or any shops were open and cleanse Whispering Falls with her incenses.

I would swear that was why Whispering Falls always had perfect weather. Never too hot, never too cold, never too rainy. Everything was perfect and exactly like it should be.

The gravel walkway around the tree house was magical. The Singing Pettles, a beautiful flower, sang with each of my steps. "Hmmm. Lalalllaaa," they chirped one-by-one. Lanterns hung down from the overlying branches above my head that guided my path.

"Eloise?" I called when I got to the end, near the gazebo. The smell of freshly-brewed tea along with two cups sat on the table along with a tiered tray of pastries.

"There you are." Eloise popped up from a row of Drowsy Daisy which happened to be Darla's favorite flower. Eloise rubbed her hands together and spread her arms out over the sides of the path as she walked up to greet me. Hot pink sprinkles of fairy dust fell from the palms of her hands over the garden rows bringing every single flower and herb to life. "I've been expecting you." She pointed to the gazebo. Her short red hair glistened in the colorful arrangement of flowers as she sped down the pathway to greet me. Her long black cloak floated behind her. The green in her emerald eyes sparkled with glee. "I thought I would have something prepared for our little visit this morning."

Eloise always knew when she was going to have company. She was always prepared and a gracious hostess.

"Tell me," she picked up the floral teapot and poured some in each cup. "What's the pleasure that brings you by?"

Twinkly lights dripped from the ceiling of the gazebo adding to the already magical effect Eloise's garden had on me and the fact she was able to bring any dead flower back to life. She was nothing short of amazing.

"Oh Eloise." There went the waterworks and I buried my head in my arms that were resting on the table. The more I wanted to talk about Mr. Prince Charming, seeing her made me think of Oscar. "Will he ever love me again?"

"June, you mustn't cry." Eloise walked over to me and stroked my hair. "He does love you."

"I mean really love me like Gerald and Petunia?" There it was. I had finally said it out loud. Everything I had ever wanted for all of my life and to see someone else get it was truly hard.

"You are happy for Gerald and Petunia, aren't you?" Eloise asked a very good question.

I dragged my head off the café table and sat up.

"I…" I had to think about her question again before I answered. "I'm jealous."

"Yes, dear, you are." She proceeded back to the other side of the table and in one swoosh, her cloak was displayed around her as she sat in the chair. "Are you feeling a little…" She searched for a word as she waved her hand in the air. "Cloudy? Yes, cloudy is a good word to describe how you might be feeling."

"Yes!" I snapped my fingers. I knew Eloise was going to help me. Feeling much better, I took one of the croissants and ate it in one bite. "But I have to say I'm blaming it on Arabella Paxton."

"The flower girl." Eloise nodded. "She's a little feisty one, but harmless."

"Harmless?" Shock covered my face. "She's far from harmless. She sent me flowers making me believe they were from Oscar. She sent Petunia orchids with my name on it which I did not send. And she and Gerald were all secretive in a little conversation they were having."

I left out the part about how she had talked Oscar into a lunch discussing security when Arabella knew perfectly well that Oscar was not a spiritualist anymore and he couldn't put a security system in any shop with a ten-foot pole. That had to be approved by the council and the work had to be done by another spiritualist. She was just trying to get her claws into him.

"She is trying to defy all the rules." I smacked my hand on the table.

"And what about you? Are you keeping up with the rules?" she asked.

"No! No she is not." Mary Lynn floated above the Peking China Rosebed. She released her crossed legs and descended to the ground. Her pointy, black-heeled, laced-up black boots clicked when her feet touched the ground. "If I'm not mistaken, you have been using ingredients banned and from the 'do not use' list while creating an illegal potion."

"I'm not creating an illegal potion." I jumped up. Mary Lynn was going to take her granddaughter's side no matter what.

"Oh?" Mary Lynn reached out and grabbed my hand. She held it up in the air. "What is this? These burns? Burns like these only happen when you are using ingredients from the 'do not use' list."

"June?" Disappointment lingered in Eloise's emerald eyes, just like it would have in Darla's. "Is this true?"

"I…" I gulped and straightened my shoulders. "I am not making an illegal potion. Oscar is no longer a spiritualist."

"He might not be a practicing spiritualist, but we could never erase his blood." Eloise shook her head like the news of my potion blew her away. "June, you are going to get yourself into hot water if you don't follow the rules of *your* village." She let me know without saying how I was the example because I was the President.

"I told you about little Miss Flowerpants." I rolled my eyes. "She is evil! Pure evil!"

Mary Lynn opened her mouth to protest, but Eloise put her hand out to stop her.

"Does your intuition tell you that?" Eloise asked.

"No." I looked away. "But what about all the stuff she has done? All the flowers and stuff?"

"What about you distributing mojo bags all over the village?" Mary Lynn had a point.

"How is your intuition?" Eloise tried hard to bring the conversation away from Arabella.

"I guess it's fine." I shrugged. I hadn't thought about it. "I haven't made anything special but for a daughter of a customer."

"Daughter of a customer?" Eloise didn't seem to be buying the story I was selling.

"Yeah, she came in. I couldn't read her needs to see if she had an underlying issue for me to make a cure for and she told me about her daughter." I could still see the look of sadness in the woman's eyes. "That's when I had the flower delivery I thought was from Oscar." My mind wandered into his deep blue eyes that I longed to have stare back at me like they had a few months ago.

"I bet you blamed them on Arabella?" Mary Lynn crossed her arms.

Eloise hushed her again.

"What about the delivery had to do with the woman?" Eloise brought me back from my thoughts.

"Oh. I had a weird vision instead of a smell that normally comes to me when I'm making a potion." I stopped for a second to recall exactly what had happened. "I was making her daughter's fertility cure and got the delivery. After the delivery I was finishing the cure when a weird vision of this greenery stem with small pink berries on it. It was needed to finish out the potion."

"Thickeris Plant?" The words left my mouth putting panic in my throat like I had never known.

"Thickeris plant?" Mary Lynn's lip pursed. "Do not use!"

"Please don't tell me it was a Thickeris Plant." Eloise words frightened me more than Mary Lynn's. "It's a banned spiritualist herb. It will cause grave harm to whoever it is intended for."

"Grave...," I swallowed the lump in my throat, "as in 'six feet under' grave?"

"When you are so jealous of something, your spiritual side will be overtaken by fear, anxiety and lack of intuition. This means that in your spirit you do not wish Petunia and Gerald great happiness."

"That means that I've got a mean spirit." I frowned. I did think I was happy for them.

"You aren't hearing me." Eloise pointed to her heart. "When you are not truly able to be happy because of jealousy, you are inflicting harm onto them subconsciously."

"So when that woman came into the shop, she needed a fertility drug for her daughter and I gave her the plant not knowing it was going to harm her?"

Slowly Eloise nodded.

"That means I have to find the woman." I felt panic rush through my bones as the woman's face appeared in my mind.

"If her daughter takes the potion, she won't have children...ever." Eloise lowered herself into the chair, her hands tense in her lap. "Plus the Thickeris Plant is full of the Vermillian Spider."

"Vermillian Spider?" I quivered. The images of the dead spiders in the jar and all the things dying around Petunia ran through my mind like a movie.

"Vermillian Spiders are the most deadly of spiders. If you even touch one and get their bodily oils on even a tip of your finger, you could possibly go into a deep coma and die."

"Who would have access to these spiders?" My mind wandered to Arabella. If the Thickeris Plant came from her, which I was sure it had, then maybe she slipped me the spiders.

"Anyone that has access to plants, herbs." Eloise swept her hands in front of us, showcasing her beautiful garden. "But they have to be harvested. They don't just show up like any old bug."

My insides gnawed with anxiety. I wanted so badly to blame everything on Arabella if only for the fact that she was hitting on Oscar, but I knew as the Village President that I had to clear that from my thought process and give her a fair shake. Why would she give me a Thickeris Plant or the Vermillian Spiders? That was what didn't make sense.

Granted she was a little snotty and not very nice when I went to welcome her to Whispering Falls, but like Darla always told me, "We are different. Not everyone is as friendly as we are June. Be nice to everyone regardless of how they treat you." And that was exactly what I was going to do. I was going to be nice to Arabella Paxton if it killed me.

"You need to find that customer using whatever means you can come up with." Mary Lynn's sweet edge turned high-pitched and reedy. Her eyes clouded with sadness.

Without her telling me, I knew she wanted me to use my spiritual gifts to find the customer.

"I told you not to do that potion," Madame Torres
blazed tightly from the bottom of my bag.

Eloise and Mary Lynn shot each other a glance. Their
eyes stirred with a depth of anger.

"You are the Village President," Eloise scolded. "How
many times are you going to get leeway, June, before they
make you step down?"

Mary Lynn swiveled her eyes upward, making it
obvious she didn't want to know what was being said
because she was one of the Order of Elders who would
impeach me.

"I...I," I stalled for time and pinched my lips together
while rubbing my tongue along the backs of my teeth. "I
will take care of this. No one got hurt. I smudged the
village. All will be good. Just let me take care of it before
you do anything."

The plea was more for Mary Lynn than Eloise. If she
didn't buy my apology, she would have to go to the Order
of Elders telling them I'm accused her granddaughter of
sabotaging me and that I used an illegal herb.

"I'm my defense." I put my hands in the air. "I did use
my intuition to use the Thickeris Plant." My mind snapped
shut and so did my mouth.

If my intuition was told to use the plant, it was solely
because I was reading the client. The short-blond-haired
woman who was styled so cute not to mention the fabulous
pair of emerald teardrop earrings she wore popped into my
head. She did know a lot about herbs and she did ask about
Luna Moth Wing. Plus she knew exactly what she was
there for...infertility. If she wanted to help her daughter
and the Thickeris Plant hit my intuition...

"I've got to go." I jumped up and grabbed my bag,
strapping it over my shoulder. The woman didn't want to

help anyone with having a baby. She wanted to prevent someone, but who?

Mr. Prince Charming was waiting by the gate ready to go.

"June! You better take care of this before something really bad happens," Eloise warned. "You can see the weather pattern is feeling some sort of effect and I can't help but wonder if it has to do with this illegal potion."

I waved my hands in the air. I didn't have time to sit here and discuss my punishment. I had to get back to Whispering Falls and figure out how to find that customer. Not to mention plan an engagement shower.

There were at least a few spurts of sun dotting through the grey sky which sent a little hope that all was not lost and I was going to be able to get back the potion.

The faster I walked, the more things didn't make sense in my head. Who was the woman? Why did she want to harm someone in such an evil way? Did this have anything to do with the weather pattern like Eloise thought? If so, was the customer a spiritualist? More importantly, why didn't my intuition clue me on the evil she had deep inside of her? What about Arabella? She had a hidden agenda and I had to figure that out too. Especially since my relationship with Oscar seemed to rely on it.

Chapter Fifteen

"Hey!" Raven wiped her floured hands down her Wicked Good apron leaving white skid marks down the front of it. "Are you needing a June's Gem fix already?" There was a twinkle of excitement in her deep eyes.

"Actually, I'm here because I wanted to see if you could come up with some party goodies pretty quickly. Like for tonight?" There was a hint of begging in my question.

"I already knew it." She pointed over to a stack of pink and green Wicked Good boxes. "It was written in the dough that I was going to get a big request this morning. I just didn't know it was for the party." She winked and went over to retrieve them.

"You can just leave them here because," I bit my lip, "I was wondering if we could do it in your little café party room after hours?"

"I'd love to." She smiled and brushed her long black hair over her shoulder.

"What's up?" Faith came around the corner with the cleaning rag and bucket in her hands. She was good at cleaning the café tables as soon as a customer got up.

"I'm planning Gerald and Petunia's engagement party." I rubbed my hands together. The clock on the wall read nine o'clock which meant A Charming Cure was supposed to be open. "Faith, do you mind working at the shop for me today so I can get all of this together?"

"Sure." She put the bucket down. I gave her the keys. "Thanks." She smiled and headed to the door. "I love getting extra cash."

"Great. I'll be by later to check on you. There are plenty of potions ready to go," I assured her. "If you need something made up, just holler for me."

She made the "aye, aye captain" signal and headed out the door.

I wrapped up my business with Raven and made my way over to The Gathering Grove. It was time I asked Gerald about his little intense conversation with Arabella.

The morning rush breakfast crowd stood in line for Gerald's amazing tea. I wiggled my way in the door and darted in and out of the line before I made my way to the front. All of Gerald's employees were busy bees, but he wasn't in the front. I was sure he was in the back steeping a tea cup to read someone's leaves.

The door to the back room swung in a little when I pushed it to go through. When I stepped in, I heard voices. I stopped and did what I wasn't supposed to do, but what any curious spiritualist would...I listened.

"You know you can't go through with this." The voice was Arabella's. She sniffed like she was crying.

"I know." Gerald sounded exhausted.

Can't go through with what? I was all ears.

"I love you. Please don't do this to me," Arabella begged him.

I love you? Dirty old man. My eyes lowered. I glared in the direction of the voices trying to decide if I let myself be known. How could he be cheating on Petunia after all of this time?

"I love you too." The sound of arms reaching around and hugging were loud and clear. "I think I'm so far into it that I can't get out of marrying her."

"I won't let you do this to us." Arabella was more threatening than helping.

Of course you won't, you little tramp.

I tiptoed a little closer and peeked around the corner of the wall. My heart dropped when I saw Arabella in

Gerald's arms. Her face was nuzzled in his neck as he stroked her long hair and kissed the top of her head.

I put my hand up to my chest to keep my heart from beating out of it. There was no way I was seeing this. I blinked several times in an attempt to make the scene go away.

"You can't marry her." Arabella was crying.

"Shh," Gerald soothed her.

I couldn't take it anymore. I rolled my eyes and disappeared back around the corner, slipping out of the back room before anyone saw me.

"Watch it!" Someone shoved me when I ran out of the shop, knocking into the front door.

"Sorry," I mumbled and found myself standing on the sidewalk outside of The Gathering Grove gasping for air. My lungs felt like someone had put a vice on them.

My eyes slowly slid over to Magical Moments. I had never wished so much evil on one person, but Arabella was proving to be a little more than Whispering Falls could handle. Was it not enough that she wanted Oscar, but also she already had her claws sunk into Gerald.

"June?" Petunia stood in front of me. Her lips were a little cracked. Clyde sat on her shoulders. His feathers gave a little color surrounding her.

"Hey," I said blankly and blinked my eyes.

"Are you okay?" She smiled. Given her appearance, I knew I had little time to figure out what was going on. She was losing her vibrancy which made me wonder if she knew about Arabella and that was why she had to get married.

"Are you okay?" I threw the question back at her. It took every ounce in my body not to drag her into The Gathering Grove and shove her through the back door so she could see her cheating fiancé for herself.

"Great!" She clasped her hands together. "Gerald has agreed to the engagement party tonight."

"Oh." I gritted my teeth. Maybe Gerald was breaking it off with Arabella and that was what I had witnessed.

"Ladies." Arabella tugged on the bottom of her shirt and swung her hair to the side when she stepped out of The Gathering Grove. "Petunia, I have some lovely flowers for the party tonight. I can't wait to show you."

I bet you can't. My eyes clung to hers, analyzing her every move.

"Wonderful. June, did you get all the other stuff together?" Petunia asked me.

"Of course I did." I decided I wasn't going to spoil anything for Petunia. I was going to give Gerald a chance to come clean, whether it was going to be to me or her. Either way, he was going to come clean and Arabella was going to be exposed.

Her negative energy had to be why the weather was off. There was no other explanation. Unless...it was my customer.

"Be at Wicked Good at eight o'clock tonight." I reached out and patted Petunia on the arm. I turned to Arabella. My voice was cold and crisp, "You can deliver your little petals yourself to Raven at Wicked Good."

Arabella drew back like I had just offended her. "Are you feeling okay June?"

"You better watch yourself," I warned in a whisper when I passed her on my way back to my shop.

A few minutes later I was standing on the stoop of A Charming Cure feeling a little bit better.

"Everything has been great," Faith assured me when I walked back to the counter where she was just finishing up with a customer. The shop was filled.

"Something terrible has happened." Madame Torres
glowed from the bottom of the bag.

"Do you mind?" I pointed around the store as I
excused myself to the back room of the shop.

"Of course I don't." Faith shrugged. Her blue eyes
widened. "I love working here."

"Great." I dismissed myself.

I reached in my bag and pulled out Madame Torres
setting her on the table. "Go on," I encouraged her, though
her eyes told me I wasn't going to like what I saw.

Like a movie, Madame Torres showed me what she
was talking about.

Gerald and Petunia were having a little spat in the back
of The Gathering Grove where moments earlier I had seen
him embracing Arabella. They were still arguing about
when they should get married. Petunia claimed they had to
do it ASAP while Gerald protested they had to wait a while
longer. Petunia grew more mad with each word he was
saying. She stomped her foot on the ground, Clyde flew off
her shoulder, more dried leaves fell out along with a bird. A
dead bird. Petunia looked down and then back at Gerald.
Her face was no longer ashen, it was a deep grey like she
was dead...she fell to the ground.

Chapter Sixteen

I rushed back to The Gathering Grove as quick as I could without a word between us. There was thick tension in the air. Something was wrong and I didn't need to see the black cloud that hung over Whispering Falls to tell me because my intuition hit my gut like someone had thrown a bowling ball at my stomach.

I pushed my way past some of the employees to find Colton Lance was already there.

"What happened?" I asked Colton.

"Not sure." He was knelt down next to her. "She's still breathing." Sirens blared causing it hard for me to hear him. "Back away!" he yelled, motioning the crowd to make way for the Karima sisters.

I stepped back and peered around the crowd that had huddled in the shop for Gerald. He was there when Madame Torres showed us what was going on, but he wasn't anywhere to be seen now. He had to be here somewhere. I twirled around to see if I could find the top hat that stuck out like a sore thumb. He would never leave Petunia. Would he?

"Where is Gerald?" I whispered to Chandra who was standing in the front of the crowd with a hanky over her mouth.

"Oh June," she wept. "Isn't this terrible?"

"Yes. Awful. Where is Gerald?" There was something not right with this entire situation. One minute Gerald and Petunia were talking, the next minute she's on the ground and her fiancé was nowhere to be seen? That definitely struck me as odd.

"I have no idea. All I know was he was demanding they keep the wedding at a later date and she refused." Chandra pointed to A Cleansing Spirit Spa. "They were so loud, I could hear them all the way down to my shop. I was working on a customer's bunions when I heard Petunia scream. Next thing I know here we are."

"Did you see Gerald?" I asked Ophelia.

"No. I heard nothing." She shrugged. "A customer came in and said there was a woman on the ground in the tea shop. That's when I called Colton."

"I said move it!" Constance Karima screeched, wheeling the gurney through the crowd, taking no prisoners if she took someone out. "Trying to save a life here people!"

Everyone parted, letting the Karimas do their thing. The crowd followed them to the street where the hearse-slash-ambulance waited.

The Karimas were good at their job—they worked like a well-oiled machine. In one swoop, they had Petunia on the gurney, strapped in, and back in the ambulance, which was really a hearse with a light, before the blink of a bat's eye.

Arabella stood next to the hearse. A tear glistened on her pale heart-shaped face. I held the image in my mind while I closed my eyes and took a deep breath. *Cough, cough.* The feelings I got from the image made me nearly pass out.

"June?" Chandra's hand was heavy on my back. "Are you okay?"

"I'm fine. I'm fine." I smiled and shook my head. I looked back over at Arabella. She was gone.

The lights rotated on the ambulance before the blare of the sirens could be heard, echoing off the mountains as the sisters threw the car in gear and took off toward Hidden Halls, A Spiritualist University Hospital. It was the closest spiritual hospital around here.

It wasn't like we could send our people to a regular hospital because sometimes we didn't have what non-spiritualists could get.

My great-aunt Helena was the dean at the University, which meant she oversaw all the hospital activities. I would definitely be getting in touch with her, especially to see if Petunia had any visitors…like Gerald.

I took one more look around to see if I saw him, but he wasn't there. Finding him and trying to figure out why Arabella was so emotional was going at the top of my list of things to check out after I talked to Colton.

"Well?" I interrupted Colton as he was writing something down in his cop notebook. His shiny nametag read "Colton Lance" in bold black letters.

He took off his hat and stuck it under his armpit. He ran his big hands through his messy blond hair. "Got me." He shrugged. "No visible signs of trauma." He hesitated like his words tentatively tested the idea of something else. "I wonder if she was poisoned."

"Poisoned?" A warning whispered in my head followed up by affirmation from my intuition. *Poisoned*? Petunia was poisoned.

Chapter Seventeen

"Something is not adding up." I paced back and forth in my family room.

Madame Torres sat on the coffee table while Mr. Prince Charming sat on my couch with his leg straight up in the air, cleaning his nether region.

"What do you mean?" Bella sat on the edge of the couch. She dangled my bracelet from her fingertips.

I walked over and let her clasp it on my wrist, feeling completely better once it was fastened and back on my body. A sense of relief crept through my bones.

Mewlll. Mr. Prince Charming turned his attention to what we were doing. He jumped up and ran to the edge of the couch next to Bella. He batted the dangling charms.

"Yes. I need all the protection I can get." I felt the charms and found the new one with the dove and circle. "But what does this mean?"

"We need to figure out what is going on around here." Bella stood up and walked over to the sink. She leaned on it, peering out the window. "The darkness has engulfed the entire town. I'm glad you canceled the party. I don't think anyone should be out in this."

Unfortunately, this was the result of evil lurking in the town and Eloise had to do a cleansing ceremony to get rid of it. Maybe two or three cleansing ceremonies.

"Gerald looks awfully suspicious," I noted.

"He does. I'm having a hard time trying to reason with the poisoning thing." Bella shook her head and turned back toward me. "I really have to get home. I don't want to be anywhere near the cleansing." She pointed out the window.

I looked.

There was a faint light going down the hill toward Whispering Falls. Eloise had her lantern on full blast as she made her way to Main Street where she would begin the lengthy process of ridding the evil from the air.

We said our goodbyes and she disappeared into the dark night.

"I have the answers you shall seek." A hazy purple glowed from Madame Torres. The closer I got, the brighter the tint.

I knelt down next to the coffee table and placed a hand on each side of her, slightly cupping the ball.

"Magic spirit of the ball show me the past. Oh magic one, show me the past I seek of Petunia Shrubwood and Gerald Regiula." Slowly I raised my hands, hovered them over the ball for a moment before I waved them in a back and forth motion.

The ball clouded with a dark red hue, almost the color of deep blood. Small bubbles burst inside the globe, making a picture of the inside of Glorybee and Petunia rushing around showing everyone her ring. The customer I had helped with her daughter's potion stood to the side watching every single move Petunia made. The look in her eyes was of disgust—almost hatred. Petunia walked over to the counter and picked up a cup of tea, "He owns The Gathering Grove. You should go and grab a cup of tea. It's the best in the south." Petunia took a sip and put the tea back. My customer walked over and looked at the tea. She glanced around before putting something in Petunia's cup.

In a blink, Madame Torres shut off.

"Shit." I bit my lip. "There is only one thing to do." I reached over to a curled-up Mr. Prince Charming, nestled on the couch pillows. "We have to go break into Glorybee to see if we can find something."

Though it was a long shot because I was sure Colton had combed the place after he locked Glorybee's door with a sign reading: *Closed Until Further Notice*.

Carefully I picked up Madame Torres and placed her back in my bag. I stood up and like he knew what I was doing, Mr. Prince Charming got up and stretched.

Meow, meow. He rubbed the side of his head on my wrist, directly on the dangling charms. If this was any other cat, I would believe it was looking for a good place to scratch. Not Mr. Prince Charming. He was warning me not to take off the bracelet.

"Don't worry." This type of caution from him meant there was imminent danger in my future and to watch my back. "You are going to be right by my side."

I stood up, put my coat on and threw the bag over my shoulder.

"Let's go." I took a deep breath along with a deep gulp before opening the door and disappearing into the abyss of darkness.

Chapter Eighteen

The chill hung over me like a thick blanket sending goose bumps all over my body. It was the first time I could recall Whispering Falls' weather being so cold. I guessed that was what evil did...bring misery to everyone in its path.

Still, the question hung around me. Why would anyone hurt Petunia? If it was my customer, who was she? Where did she come from?

"Could it be any colder?" I flipped up the collar up on my red coat to protect my face from the whipping wind that tore into me like I had pissed it off.

Even Mr. Prince Charming looked cold and he had enough fur on him to make two sweaters. He shot out ahead of me, making it difficult for me to see. In the distance I could see the slow swing of light, to and fro, taking comfort in knowing that I was headed in the right direction—not to mention I wouldn't be alone in the village. Eloise's incense filled the evil night air.

I made my way to the back of Glorybee where Petunia used the back door to get into her apartment situated behind the shop. Mr. Prince Charming waited for me just inside the frame.

"You have to make sure the animals stay calm while I snoop around." It was very clear why he had to come with me. He had spent so much time there, the animals knew him better than me. Plus I couldn't risk them going nuts when I intruded on their territory, sending them into a flurry of frenzy, which could be heard outside of the pet store.

Many times something would go wrong and I could hear the displeasure of Clyde while I was in A Charming Cure.

I pulled out a pen from deep within my bag and unscrewed the barrel to get the small thin plastic ink tube out. This was a trick I had learned from Oscar when we were kids. He could break into anywhere, any lock by veraciously rubbing the plastic between the palms of his hands to heat up the ink, then breaking the plastic in half letting the hot ink ooze into the hole of the lock. This allowed the lock to heat up enough that anything you stuck in there would easily open it.

And it still worked like a charm. I ran my hand up the dark wall before I shut the door behind me. The light switch was on the right side and I flipped it on. Clyde's cage was to the right, but it was empty. The small kitchenette was as clean as a whistle, which surprised me since she was always surrounded by animals. There didn't seem to be any drink glasses out, let alone the one Madame Torres had shown me in the crystal ball. That was the one I was on a mission to get.

The first place to look would be the counter in the shop. Madame Torres was good about leading me to exactly where I needed to go, even if I was a few hours too late to save Petunia.

I took my cell phone out of my bag so I could use the flashlight feature. If Colton or even Eloise saw a light on in the shop, they would surely be there to investigate.

Slowly I opened the door between Petunia's living space and the shop, just enough to get an eyeball full of shop. It was dark and quiet like I expected. The large front windows showed a perfect view of Main Street. The carriage lights, though the light was somewhat dismal from the evil fog that had seemed to set in, did illuminate enough to see Eloise was walking away from the shop and toward the other end of Main Street near Two Sisters and a Funeral.

The small cell phone flashlight was perfect for what I
needed. Mr. Prince Charming did his thing keeping the
animals quiet while I nosed around.

Who, who. The owl sat at the top of the tree with one
eye opened. He was definitely keeping that one eye on me.
A couple of birds soared through the air and did a couple of
dive bombs in my direction to see what I was doing. There
was sadness in the air, making it hard to breathe or maybe
it was my nerves making me heave in and out. I was hoping
there was something, anything to clue me in on what had
happened to Petunia and why Gerald hadn't been seen
since. And if I could find the cup, I could tell if my
customer had messed with it.

Mewl. Mr. Prince Charming was a little more quiet
than normal. I could see his long white tail sticking up in
another aisle, like a white flag waving in the night. I rushed
over to see what he was doing and shined the flashlight in
his direction before he darted off.

The potion bottle I had given the customer for her
daughter's fertility was lying on its side on one of the
shelves with the lid off. Carefully I picked it up and looked
in it. The potion was gone.

Mewl. Mr. Prince Charming was across the room at the
counter. I slipped the potion bottle in my bag and went over
to see what else he had found for me.

"The cup," I whispered and gave him a little scratch
behind his ears. "Good boy."

I shined the flashlight in the tea cup that'd had
Gerald's tea that Petunia had boasted about. It was empty
too, but there was a little ring of dried, leftover tea on the
bottom. Enough to get a sample.

Mewl.

I slipped the cup in my bag and went to the front of the store where Mr. Prince Charming hunkered down in front of the window.

"Good idea." I got on my knees and began to crawl toward him. The risk of someone watching the window at Glorybee was highly likely and I didn't want to be seen. Madame Torres glowed causing the fabric of my bag to light up. Quickly I crawled behind one of the shelves before taking her out.

"Gerald's fortune is written in the stars. His past is in the galaxy trying to get out on the full moon..." Madame Torres drifted off. The glass ball showed Gerald sitting on a bed with his head in his lap, visibly crying. Madame Torres's cold grey eyes appeared. They matched the evil fog that was still blanketing all of Whispering Falls. "The past is near. The answers you seek are far, far away in the Village of Azarcabam. Fear. June Heal, fear."

Madame Torres went black.

"Hold on," I whispered, shaking her back and forth trying to get her to come back. "Fear? Fear what?"

Mewl.

This time Mr. Prince Charming was a bit more urgent.

"Uh." I put Madame Torres back in the bag and continued back on my journey on my hands and knees to find Mr. Prince Charming. "I'm going to have to look up this Azarwhatchamacallit."

I couldn't say the name, much less remember it.

"What did she mean his past? Gerald has a past?" As far as I knew, Gerald had always lived in Whispering Falls. I hadn't been here long. Whispering Falls was like every other city in Kentucky and it wasn't exempt from idle gossip. I would have heard something about a shady past if he had one.

"I don't know. That is why I called you." Colton was right outside of the shop door standing on Main Street talking to someone. "I wouldn't say June had anything to do with it, but she has been awfully strange since they got engaged this morning."

"I saw her a couple of times and she seemed fine," Oscar's voice was resigned.

My mouth flew open. Mr. Prince Charming put his paw on my hand, since I was still in a crawling position. He knew I was about to lose it. I eased myself down and sat cross-legged with my ear to the door. Why on earth did Colton call Oscar about me? And what was he worried about?

"Several members of the community said she fainted when she saw Gerald propose to Petunia. Arabella said she was there when they were trying to wake June. Petunia was telling them how June was jealous that she wasn't getting married to you."

"Me?" Oscar sounded shocked.

I let out a small sigh and lowered my head.

"Yea and that she had been running all around the town doing who knows what," Colton paused.

"What about the fiancé? Gerald?" Oscar asked some great questions. That should be the number one suspect on everyone's mind, not me.

"He checks out fine. He went to be with Petunia at the hospital." Colton thought he knew everything. But he didn't have a Madame Torres. Gerald was far from the hospital and I was going to find out why.

"And the ring."

"Petunia's ring?"

"Yea. Supposedly it was the ring June had picked out to get for her own engagement," Colton told Oscar all the truth about me, but it wasn't like I would ever do anything to hurt Petunia.

"Who is telling you all this?" Oscar was on to his detective work.

"Arabella Paxton."

Arabella. My eyes lowered. Arabella was framing me. But why? And what did she have to do with Gerald?

In that instant, I knew I had to go to Azarcabam to seek the answers before I could ever come back to Whispering Falls.

Chapter Nineteen

"How on earth did I become a suspect?" I stomped back up the hill. Mr. Prince Charming making strides next to me had to bear the brunt of my tyrant. "They can't possibly think I had anything to do with it."

Grrr, Mr. Prince Charming let me know his displeasure.

"Okay. Fine." I glanced back to make sure no one had seen me slip out of the back of Glorybee and followed me. Petunia was on my list to see next. Well, really I wanted to see my great-aunt Helena. They had a terrific forensic lab run by the best spiritual wizards. They would be able to figure out if the customer had accidentally put my potion in Petunia's cup or if there was an intention behind it. Maybe she didn't use the potion at all. Maybe my customer had nothing to do with this and the potion got spilled by one of the animals living in the pet shop. How did Arabella play into all of this? I had a sneaky suspicion she had a key role in Gerald skipping town.

There were a lot of maybes and I had to get to the bottom of it. The more time away from Whispering Falls, the more time Arabella could hatch her evil plan to get Oscar or worse…do more harm on Whispering Falls.

The crackling of leaves made me move a little quicker. Mr. Prince Charming's tail made it much easier for me to see even though the fog had gotten thicker the closer we got to the wooded area behind my cottage. Hidden Halls, A Spiritualist University Hospital wasn't the easiest of places to get to on foot. But that was how everyone but the Teletransporters got there. Often times I wished I had a really cool spiritual gift like teletransporting and this was one of those times.

"We have to hurry." A creeping uneasiness tugged at the bottom of my heart.

Without looking back, Mr. Prince Charming and I hurried to the wheat field beyond the wooded area. Like always, the wheat parted giving us a little path that would lead us to the wooden sign that had several long wooden arms, each with a finger pointing in a different direction.

"Eye of Newt Crystal Ball School, Tickle Palm School, Intuition School," I read the down the arms until I saw exactly what I needed. "There it is, Hospital."

I reached up and tapped the finger pointing to the hospital. Like magic, a pathway appeared across the wheat field.

My eyes followed as the path gained momentum and ended at a Hidden Halls, A Spiritualist University Hospital sign. Mr. Prince Charming darted ahead. I wasn't too far behind. If my intuition was right and I was pretty sure it was, Oscar was trying to get in touch with me to question me about Petunia.

Uh, I groaned. Colton was such a pansy that he had to put Oscar up to questioning me when it wasn't even Oscar's jurisdiction. Even if they did try to pin Petunia's poisoning on me, if that was what she had, then by Rule Number Five I couldn't be arrested until all the facts were in. The only thing I couldn't do was what I was doing now. Leave.

Yep. The rule states that I can't be arrested and I can't leave until it's solved. That could be years in the spiritual world.

The sliding glass doors of the hospital opened when the sensory detected me coming. The receptionist sat at the desk with her body hunched over her computer. Her tight curls sat on her head like a brill-o pad and her small red-framed glasses made her eyes magnified, slightly scaring me a little bit.

"State your business." She was serious.

"Petunia Shrubwood," I stated my business. Mr. Prince Charming sat down next to my feet.

"Dang!" She smacked her desk. "This computer candy game is killing me. Did you say Petun—" She lifted her head away from her computer screen. She eyed me over the top of the red frames.

"Yes." There was a little tension between her question and my answer. Something told me that she was on alert for anyone who was trying to get in to see Petunia.

"Name?" She grabbed a folder from the front drawer of her desk.

"June Heal." I rubbed my wrist where my charm bracelet dangled, *please let Petunia be okay.*

She flipped the folder open and slid her finger down the first piece of paper in it. "June. June," she repeated as her eyes descended down the paper. She tapped it. "June Heal." She looked back up at me. "June Heal," she confirmed. She stood up and looked over the counter to my feet. "You must be Mr. Prince Charming."

Meow, meow.

I wondered what the little paper said about me and my fairy-god cat, but didn't care when she sent me into the elevator behind her. It wasn't a regular hospital elevator.

I stepped in. The stainless steel box didn't have any buttons in it to push, nor did it have an escape hatch on top, which was the first thing I looked for in case I had to make a quick exit. Again…another reason I wished to have a cool teletransporting gift. No such luck.

I took my bag off my shoulder and stuck it on the other one. Madame Torres was lit up. She had some news. I hoped it was something I could use and not the cryptic stuff she handed me last time.

The elevator shot down instead of up and zigzagged right and then left, leaving me a little dizzy. I held on to my bag. The doors opened and I stepped out into a dark room. The only thing I could see was Madame Torres.

I took her out and put her up to my face.

Holding her with one hand, I waved my other hand over her.

"Magic spirit of the ball, show me Gerald past and all."

"The past of Gerald is what you seek. Beware of gypsy for she is not meek." Madame Torres glowed with a picture of Gerald still sitting with his head buried in his hands. A gypsy in a black veil appeared. Coins dangled from the hood on the veil covering her forehead. Madame Torres zeroed in on the gypsy eyes. The liner was thick, black and heavy just like her black eyes.

Madame Torres went black. I waved my hand again in hopes she'd give me something more, but she didn't. All of this dark magic was draining her and me too.

"I wondered when you would be coming here." The voice came before the purple smoke filled the space.

"Hello Aunt Helena." Finally. Someone who could help me.

The purple smoke gave way to lights, exposing Aunt Helena. She swung around in her pointy red boots, sending her cape behind her. The cape snapped. Petunia appeared in a hospital bed behind her. It was not the usual bed you see in the hospital with the hard mattress, steel sides and million little buttons for the TV, nurse, up and down. Petunia floated on a fluff of cotton clouds, at least that was what they reminded me of. There were no tubes. She was enclosed in glass.

I dug down into my bag and pulled out the potion, along with the tea cup. I held it out for her to take. "Here is what I collected from Glorybee Pet Shop."

"Do you want to tell me about the ingredients you have been using?" The lines around her eyes creased. Displeasure hung around her mouth.

"I guess you saw Mary Lynn." I hung my head. There was nothing worse than getting scolded by my aunt, much less the dean of the biggest university in the spiritual world.

"Yes. I told her I would speak with you. Then this happened." She drew her hands from under her cloak and swept one arm across, exposing her long thin hands and long red nails as she gestured toward Petunia.

"That is not my fault."

"Let's hope not." She slid her arm my way and held her palm upward. Carefully I put the potion bottle and tea cup in her hand. She curled them into a ball before slipping them into the pocket of her cloak. "Now." She clasped her hands back in front of her. "Tell me about this situation."

She didn't have to say another word. I knew exactly what she was talking about. Petunia. The potion.

"I don't really know, but I do know Arabella Paxton is trying to frame me for it." The nerve of her. Wild thoughts ran through my head which I kept to myself because Aunt Helena didn't care about silly things.

"Let's start with the Thickeris Plant. Where did it come from?" She wasn't going to beat around the bush.

"Arabella."

"Arabella Paxton, Mary Lynn's granddaughter gave you Thickeris Plant?" she mocked me. Her voice held heavy sarcasm.

"Well we had just had a little tiff about following the rules. She hit on Oscar and pretty much warned me that she was going to steal him away from me," I stated the facts.

"Is it a coincidence that she just opened Magical Moments, a flower shop?"

Aunt Helena was old, but she was far from stupid. Her eyes narrowed, leaving a dark shadow down her cheeks. I didn't know if it was the dark, scary room that put a little fright in my soul or if it was Aunt Helena, but I knew I had little time to spend there before Colton would figure out where I had gone.

"That would be a little too obvious." Aunt Helena swept her cloak in a twirl and glided over to Petunia. "I'm assuming you want me to send the tea cup to forensics to see if someone used your potion to try to kill Petunia?"

"Madame Torres has been showing me some strange turns of events." I walked over and looked at Petunia. She looked as if she was peacefully sleeping in her glass box. "First she showed Petunia giving everyone in her store a good look at her ring. In the background my customer—the one I gave the fertility potion to that included the Thickeris—she slipped by the crowd gathered around Petunia and had her back to Madame Torres's perspective. It looked like she put something in Petunia's tea cup. It was right after that Petunia went down."

"Hmm." Aunt Helena was engaged in what I had to say. "Go on."

"That is all about my customer. Then I saw Gerald and Arabella secretly talking to each other. Neither of them looked happy with the other." I walked around the glass box to Petunia's head. The leaves still looked like they were dying, which made me worry she wasn't getting better with the oxygen they were pumping into her. "Before any of this, Petunia noticed things around her were dying." I pointed to her head. "She knew something was wrong. So much so that she would have married Gerald right on Main Street after he proposed if he would have agreed to it."

"He didn't want to?"

"No. He refused to rush it." I placed my hands on my stomach. With my eyes closed I took a deep breath. It was time for me to go.

"That is strange since they have been together all this time." Aunt Helena drummed her fingers together. She looked into the distance, hopefully taking in everything I was telling her and weighing the facts.

"Plus Gerald skipped town right after Petunia passed out." That was an important part not to leave out. I rushed my words, "Madame Torres showed Gerald extremely upset in the Village of Azarcabam."

Aunt Helena drew in a lengthy gasp. Slowly her eyes slid up to mine. They were deep, dark and scared. It wasn't a look I had ever seen in her eyes. Chills covered my entire body. I was scared to the core.

"You will not go to the Village of Azarcabam. That is final!" The ground shook when Aunt Helena stomped her foot on the ground, making it crystal clear that she didn't approve.

"I don't have a choice." My voice was fragile and shaky. My entire body shook. There had never been a time I had gone against Aunt Helena. "I'm going to be arrested for this." I tried to steady my trembling finger when I pointed it directly at Petunia.

"Tell me," Aunt Helena swept across the floor and stood next to me. She took my hands in hers. My hands were freezing. She gently rubbed them. "You will not be safe there. The Village of Azarcabam is not a spiritualist community. It's full of heathens that are looking for people like us."

"Gerald is there. He is not evil or bad, but he is there because he knows something. Something that is going to save me."

Rowl! Mr. Prince Charming darted around the room. "I have to go." I watched Mr. Prince Charming. He was telling me it was time to go. They were getting closer to finding me to bring me in for questioning. I rubbed my charm bracelet. "Mr. Prince Charming will keep me safe. Madame Torres will keep me posted of anything evil coming my way."

My eyes clung to Aunt Helena as I tried to analyze what she was thinking.

I continued, "Colton will be here soon. If I'm here, he will take me in for questioning and I won't be able to leave Whispering Falls." I squeezed her hands before I pulled mine away. "Please trust me. After all, I did learn my gift from the best." My trembling lips created a shaky smile.

After living in Whispering Falls for a few months, I had gone to Hidden Halls, A Spiritualist University to help hone my magical skills. She was not only the dean and my great-aunt, she was my teacher.

"Go! Now!" She twisted her cape around her followed by a puff of purple smoke and she was gone.

Rowl! Mr. Prince Charming ran over to the elevator and jumped in. Without hesitating I followed and let the elevator descend to the first floor.

The receptionist was not there.

Mewl. Mr. Prince Charming stopped at the hospital sliding doors when he saw I was not following him. *Mewwwl.*

"I know I have limited time, but I have to check the guest registry." I pulled open the desk drawer where the receptionist had pulled Petunia's file from.

Confidential was written big and bold in red on the front of it. I opened it up. The first page was a list of approved visitors along with their photos. Then there was me.

"June Heal. Village President of Whispering Falls. Niece of Dean Helena Heal. She can visit with detailed security. If she visits, do not stop her. Call Colton Lance, sheriff of Whispering Falls immediately. Order of Colton Lance." Baffled, I looked up at Mr. Prince Charming.

How could they possibly think I was so jealous that I would hurt Petunia? How could they believe Arabella over me? Not that she had lied. I did do all those things. But they were never done out of hatred or out of malice.

Rowwwl. He darted out of the hospital, telling me I better get going.

Quickly I put the file back in the drawer where I found it. I made sure no one was around before I headed out the door.

Uh! The wind got knocked out of me like I'd been socked. Trying to catch my breath, I took a deep inhale. The stillness of the night hit my gut. I darted behind the shrubbery outside of the hospital doors just in time.

"I'm at the hospital. The receptionist told me June was here to see Petunia. Can you get a hold of the dean?" Colton snapped his phone shut and walked into the hospital.

"Just in time." I stood up and watched him walk up to the receptionist desk. The receptionist was there sipping on a cup of coffee, which was where she must have been when I left.

A few words were exchanged between the two of them.

"Is she still there?" Colton's voice came from my bag. I opened it. Madame Torres glowed like fire as Colton's conversation came through her like a speaker.

I looked in the doors and the receptionist touched the beach picture hanging behind her. Instantly it showed Petunia in the glass box. No one was there. Including me.

"Where is she?" Colton demanded to know.

The receptionist spit a little bit of her coffee out of her mouth.

"She was here." The woman swept her finger across the screen, rewinding the video. The only images it showed was Aunt Helena checking on Petunia. There wasn't any sign of me or Mr. Prince Charming being there. "I swear she was here."

"You're welcome." Madame Torres showed Aunt Helena's face. "Go!"

Aunt Helena had erased the security tape, giving me a little time to try to figure out exactly what had happened to Petunia.

"Get the tea cup tested," I whispered into the globe before I stuck Madame Torres deep within my bag and headed out on my long destination to Azarcabam.

Chapter Twenty

"This should be fun." I stood at the wooden arm in the wheat field trying to figure out exactly which way I needed to go to get to Azarcabam. It wasn't like I could go to the airport or bus station and check departure times.

Plus I had never ventured any further than the city limits of Locust Grove or Whispering Falls. I had to rely on my intuition and magic to get me there.

Meow. Mr. Prince Charming's long white tail was like a finger and pointed to the wooden sign. There was a new finger added with the picture of a train.

"I guess we are going on a train ride." I reached out and touched the arm. Like magic, the wheat field parted, exposing an old locomotive.

"All aboard for Azarcabam!" The conductor hung out of the engine window.

Wooh, wooh! The train whistle screamed. Steam blew from underneath the big hunk of metal.

"I guess he means us." Looking around, I shrugged because there was no one there but us.

There was only one passenger car attached to the engine. The big heavy doors slid open and some stairs lit up, giving Mr. Prince Charming a way to get on.

Mr. Prince Charming wasted no time and darted up the steps.

I looked back toward the wooden sign and the direction of Whispering Falls. There was a tug at my heart. I couldn't imagine leaving Oscar Park behind, but I knew if we were ever going to have a chance at a future, I was going to have to do this.

The train didn't wait until we were seated before the metal wheels began to turn, causing the shrill noise of hot metal on hot metal. The door slammed shut right as Mr.

Prince Charming and I took a seat on one of the two red velvet benches. Mr. Prince Charming curled up and closed his eyes.

I wanted to do the same thing, but I was afraid to close my eyes in fear of not knowing what was going to happen. There were red velvet window shades down both sides of the passenger car. Mini tassels hung in a v-formation on the edge of each of them. If I wasn't so sure I was in present day, I'd thought I had traveled back into the 1800's.

I held tight at the train creaked back and forth. Mr. Prince Charming wasn't disturbed one bit. His head bobbled back and forth, but his eyes were shut tight. Maybe I should have woken him up to watch me as I slept, but I didn't. I figured he needed his sleep to keep me safe from harm.

I pulled on one of the shades, making it zip up and flap against the glass window. I peered outside. Everything was zooming by, but in the distance I could see a large castle on a hill. The ground was covered with thick snow. Something I was not used to. Whispering Falls' climate was strange and comfortable all year around, even though Kentucky had every single season.

When customers commented on how the weather was, we responded by saying we were having an unseasonably strange weather pattern moving through the valley.

Not Azarcabam. It looked like it was cold, very cold. I wasn't dressed for it. Looking at the snow sent a deep chill in my bones.

Thoughts of Oscar filled my head. Oscar the spiritualist would have loved this little adventure. He would be trying his hardest to clear my name. I shoved images of him out of my head. There was no time to daydream. The more time wasted, the more time I had to spend looking for

Gerald and getting back to Whispering Falls to derail anything Arabella had planned for my hunk of a man.

I pulled the shade back down. The tassels swayed with every turn of the train wheels. Suddenly it stopped. Everything stopped. The noise of the wheels, the tassels hitting the glass, the creak of the metal. Mr. Prince Charming jumped up. His eyes caught mine. We were both silent. He eased himself off the bench and sat by the door.

I lifted the edge of the shade. It was pitch black.

"Come on!" There was a tap on the window. "Get out!" The voice was gruff, not to mention scary. ""I said get out!"

The door flew open and the stairs appeared. There were no lights to light my way like there were last time.

"I said get out of my house!" The gruff voice was screaming and beating the window.

Mr. Prince Charming took off down the steps and I wasn't too far behind. He darted behind an old barrel alight with fire. The smoke flew up in the air along with the flames. Men in black cloaks, mustaches, top hats, and dark lined eyes stood around it warming their hands as bellows of laughter shook their bodies.

"Well, well." One of them turned and eyed me. "What do we have here?"

I looked back at the passenger train car. There wasn't a trace of it. Only a wooden shack and a man beating on the window with a cane screaming.

"You must be new in town." The man grinned, exposing holes where teeth should have been.

I looked down. I didn't fit in with the jeans and t-shirt I had put on to go to work in. I grabbed my bag and held it close to me, trying to keep warm from the falling snow.

"We can scoot over and give you a little warmth."
Their laughter filled the air around me. I had never been so
scared in my life.

Out of the corner of my eye I saw Mr. Prince
Charming dart into an old wooden building.

"Thief!" A couple of men stood around another barrel,
their guns strapped on their hips. They screamed at another
man as they took his head and pushed in deep into the
barrel full of water. Holding him under after they continued
to scream, "Thief!"

The men were dressed in brown pants, brown vests,
and stripped button-down shirts. They all wore a top hat.
Their eyes were lined as if they all wore makeup and each
one had a mustache. The women wore long black cloaks
and veils to cover their heavily blackened-lined eyes. Some
had jewels dangling around their foreheads like the tassels
on the train shades, and some had none.

I definitely stood out like a sore thumb.

I wasn't sure if it was night or day. All I knew was that
it was dark and I wouldn't be safe unless I slipped out of
sight into the dark shadows alongside the old buildings. I
inched my way to where I had seen Mr. Prince Charming
go, taking in all the sights along the street. There didn't
seem to be any order in the village as everyone sort of
rushed around.

There was an eerie suspicion in my gut that someone
other than the drifters around the fire barrel knew I was
there. I glanced around, but the shadow was pitch black. I
couldn't even see my hand before me. I continued in the
darkness with my eyes on the small glowing lights. They
were in the direction where Mr. Prince Charming had run
off to. It was obviously where Gerald was and Mr. Prince
Charming was getting me there.

A wind blasted past me, catching the nape of my neck, nipping me with a bite of cold. It was enough to get me moving and moving fast.

The doors of the old building swung inward when I pushed my way past the drunkards gathered on the floor at the opening. The foul air of sour whiskey and cigarettes filled my lungs.

Bar? I looked around. The old saloon was filled with men clanking their pewter goblets and drinking to anything they could possibly wrap their drunk minds around. Mr. Prince Charming stood at the top of the old wooden steps that were clear across the room. Our eyes met.

"Geez, couldn't make this any easier could you?" I groaned, trying to stay along the wall, sight unseen. This didn't seem like the place I wanted to be if someone saw me. There wasn't anyone around here who looked like me and I surely didn't want my head stuffed down into a bucket full of water like the guy I saw in the street.

I was here for one reason only. To find and question Gerald. Evidently I was in the right place because Mr. Prince Charming had led me here.

I hurried up the steps figuring the drunken men below couldn't follow me because their vision had to have been blurred with the way they were carrying on.

There was a hallway branching to the right and left once I got to the top of the steps. I saw the tip of Mr. Prince Charming's tail turn the corner down the left hall. I followed him into the open door around the corner.

The room looked like the same room Madame Torres had shown me—only it was trashed. The small bed was overturned, the little wooden desk was in pieces on the floor with what looked like the remains of the chair that had matched it.

"I hope Gerald escaped this." I looked around.

There were voices coming from down the hall. I disappeared behind the door.

"Did he really think he was going to get away with it?" The woman cackled. "We will see about that Gerald Regiula." The voice was familiar.

I peeked my head around the door when I heard the footsteps pass. They were dressed in head-to-toe black and veiled like the other women I had seen in the streets.

"This must have just happened." I stepped out from behind the door and took a good long look around the room. Mr. Prince Charming ducked his head from the overturned bed. "I wonder what they were talking about?" I rubbed my hand around my wrist, feeling all of my protective charms.

They had obviously taken Gerald against his own will, at least that was what the room looked like, but where did they take him?

I tiptoed across the room and looked out the tiny window. Barrels of fire could be seen all over the dark city. The only thing lit up was the castle-looking building way up on the hill.

"I don't think I can do this right now." Suddenly my eyes felt very heavy. I slid down the wall and landed on my butt. Mr. Prince Charming sat straight as an arrow with his face to the door.

"Do you think you could keep a watch while I…," I was going to say rest my eyes, but I did more than that.

Chapter Twenty One

The sound of claps, tambourines, hoots and hollers, along with a lot of foot stomping woke me up.

"Oh," I sighed, rubbed my eyes and remembered where I was. "Azarcabam."

Meow.

Mr. Prince Charming was still sitting in the same spot that I recalled before I had drifted off to sleep. The sky was still dark and I was no closer to finding Gerald than I was before. He looked at me before he ran out of the room, not giving me any time to really wake up and adjust to my current situation.

After a few more hoots and hollers, the music started, leaving me a little curious to what was going on.

With my hand planted firmly on the ground, I pushed myself up to my feet, but not before looking down to see what I had touched.

"Gerald." I grabbed the vintage ring, *my vintage ring.* "Petunia."

It was a sure sign Gerald was here. The first real sign since I had been here. Why did he have the ring?

I bit my lip trying to remember if I saw the ring on Petunia's finger while she was in the hospital, but I couldn't recall.

The sounds of fiddles brought me out of my thought process. I slipped the ring in my bag and slung the bag over my shoulder before I headed out to find Gerald.

Carefully I eased down the hall behind Mr. Prince Charming. The saloon was empty. There was a basket of old bread sitting on the bar next to a lot of empty whiskey jars.

"I'm starving." I grabbed the stale bread and stuffed it into my mouth. I tried not to think about who or what had touched the loaf, but desperate times called for desperate measures. And I was in a desperate time. I needed all the energy I could get in order to finish my business here.

I rolled up on my toes to look out of the swinging bar doors. The crowd had gathered around a group of gypsy dancers. The women wore chains of gold jewelry around their necks, bangle bracelets up to their elbows, and long dangling earrings. Their long brown hair hung loosely around their faces in large curls. The fiddlers were all men in balloon pants that were tapered around their ankles. Their bare feet stomped on the ground as they yelled out, never once stopping the bow as it shrilled along the fiddle strings.

The women twirled around. Their pink skirts kicked up puffs of dirt as they skimmed the dirt ground.

Dirt ground? I looked around after I realized all the snow was gone and I wasn't freezing as much.

I slipped out of the doors and into the shadows. I stuck out like a sore thumb.

"Did you hear about the visitor?" I heard one of the gypsy women talking to the other as they watched their friends dance around in a circle as some of the men passed a chair with a man sitting in it clapping his hands in the air.

I leaned a little closer to the women. If they were talking about Gerald, maybe I could get a clue on where to find him.

"She's dressed in boy pants," one of them said.

Boy pants? I glanced down. They were talking about me. I slipped back into the shadow and watched as each of them clapped, danced and yelped. There was only one way to fit in.

I eyed the roadside makeshift stand where a few of the other gypsies were selling pieces of their clothing.

Making my way around the building and staying under cover, I knew I had to get my hands on one of those outfits if I was ever going to be able to come out of the darkness and walk among them so I could find Gerald.

I dug my hand deep in my bag and searched for money. I pulled out a twenty before handing it to the woman at the booth.

"Your paper is no good to me." She scoffed. Her lips snarled. "I will take him." Her long black fingernail extended past me and pointed to something behind me.

I turned.

Hiss, hiss. Mr. Prince Charming curled his back up and showed his teeth.

The woman threw her head back in a fit of laughter before her face suddenly became serious. "Intruder!" she screamed and pointed to me.

I ran back behind the building to get out of the way of the people running after me and tripped on a cloth. I pulled the black fabric over my head until the stampede had passed me. Slowly I pulled it off my head and just below my eyes to make sure it was all clear.

A hand touched my shoulder, another one covered my mouth, nearly making me jump out of my skin.

"Shh," the woman whispered, "come with me."

There wasn't much I could do. If I didn't go with her, she might turn me in. So I went with her hoping she didn't.

Chapter Twenty Two

The fully-clothed woman was dressed in head-to-toe black. She wore a veil to cover her face. She must have been a wealthy member in the village of Azarcabam because lots of gold coins dangled down her forehead and down the length of her entire veil.

She led me into a dark room that was covered in deep purple fabrics with lots and lots of tassels dangling from everywhere. She turned on a couple of table lamps which only gave a shadow of light from the frosted globes.

"Please sit." She gestured toward the ground where there was a large area rug with big pillows thrown about. "Put your paper money on the plate."

I reached forward. With my hand over the gold plate on the small table, I uncurled my fist and let the twenty-dollar bill drop before I sat on the ground with one of the large pillows under me.

She handed me a dark jar of something with a cork on the lid.

"Drink," she encouraged me. My eyes adjusted to the light and her eyes caught mine. There was something vaguely familiar about her. That was impossible. I had never met a gypsy nor had I been out of Locust Grove or Whispering Falls.

I blew it off thinking she looked like all the other women in this community.

"It will make you feel better." She handed me a basket full of bread.

Reluctantly I reached out and held the heavy bottle. I grabbed the bread and devoured every crumb and took a few swigs of the water she handed me. Mr. Prince Charming didn't alert me to any danger as he sat next to me with his eye on the gypsy the entire time.

The gypsy danced around the room with incense in her hands. She twirled her wrists in a counter-clockwise motion two times before changing the direction to clockwise. The smoke filled the room.

I fanned my hand in front of me. The gypsy could take some lessons on how to properly use the incense from Eloise, but I wasn't here for that.

After scarfing up all the bread and after I finished off the bottle of water, I realized the gypsy sat on the arm of a big wooden chair, her legs apart with her elbows resting on them. She leaned over, her long hair dangling down in front of her. She left the veil attached around her face. Her eyes slanted, telling me she was smiling underneath her guarded face.

"What?" I asked. The image of her eyes nagged me. I dug deep in my memory to try to figure out where I knew her from.

"It's interesting to watch foreigners come into our land. But you are not just any foreigner are you?"

"I'm looking for a friend." There wasn't much more I wanted to tell her. Especially after I was warned by Madame Torres and Aunt Helena that gypsies had a strange way.

"The past is what you seek." She clapped her hands to the side. A puff of smoke swirled around her making more food to appear. She pushed the plate toward me using the tip of her toe—her dirty toe. Mr. Prince Charming pounced, standing between me and the plate.

"I'll pass." I waved it off, even though the added cheese looked divine and made my mouth water.

"Who is the man you wish to connect with?" she asked as if she were reading my mind.

"My friend, Gerald. The love of his life is gravely ill in a hospital and I must tell him." I didn't really know what the gypsy did and didn't know about me and why I was here. All I knew was that she somehow could read little bits and pieces of my mind. And I had a sneaky suspicion she knew more than she was letting on.

"Love of his life?" She drew in a breath. "That must not be true."

"How do you know? They are engaged to be married." I tucked my bag in closer to me knowing the ring was deep inside.

"How do you know this man didn't want to marry and he hurt her himself?" The gypsy asked the same question I was wanting to ask Gerald myself. She nudged the plate of food closer to me.

"When I find him, maybe I'll ask him the same question." I shook my head. "No thank you."

"Then you must take this to use or you will not find the answers your heart desires." Her hand swooped in the air creating another puff of smoke, this time grey, exposing a cloak and veil for me to use in the community.

"I can't take that." I shook my head. My intuition told me I couldn't and if I did, I would be in debt to her.

"You aren't taking it." She stood up and grabbed the sleeves of the cape, flipping it up in the air, snapping it to form. "You paid for it." She pointed to the plate where I put my paper money. "See." Her heavy brows lifted.

"Really? Twenty dollars?" I couldn't help but glance over at the veil. The deep purple teardrop gems around the veil sparkled leaving me with a wanting deep in my heart. I had always been partial to purple.

"Go on," she encouraged me. "Try it on."

Mewl. Mr. Prince Charming let me know his displeasure.

"It's not going to hurt." I shrugged and got up off the floor.

I lifted the veil up. The gems were magical. Beautiful. "Thank you." I lifted the veil up and over my head. It fit perfect.

Mr. Prince Charming was beside himself. He ran around the room as if he was looking for an exit. His tail hit a jar, knocking it to the ground. Spiders trickled everywhere.

My eyes adjusted to the label. *Vermillian Spiders.*

I gulped. Instantly I recalled where I had seen her. In A Charming Cure. I had found the customer, only I think she found me.

"You don't have a very smart friend." The gypsy laughed and pulled one of the large tapestries that hung on the wall to the side. There was a small door, big enough for a cat to run through. Mr. Prince Charming saw his opportunity and he took it, leaving me alone.

"I guess I better be on my way." My stomach knotted, instantly making me feel sick with the decision I had made putting on the cloak and veil. I had to gather my wits and decide what my next move was going to be. Madame Torres and Aunt Helena had already warned me about the gypsy ways. I was nowhere near prepared to confront her. Yet.

Get out there. Blend in. Find Gerald. Take off cloak. I had to keep repeating to make myself feel better.

"Well thanks." I didn't bother glancing back at the gypsy. I rushed out the door I had come in, leaving her and the memories of her behind. There was no time. I had to find Gerald.

The sun was shining. It was the first time I had seen the sun in a while. What was left of the snow was all gone. The castle on the hill was even scarier in the daylight.

The streets of Azarcabam were filled with all sorts of merchants and their wooden buggy carts. They pushed their wares through the streets, screaming at people to get out of their way.

The dangling gems kept beating me in the forehead, causing me to sling my head to the side as if they were side bangs.

"I wasn't finished with you yet." The familiar gypsy voice whispered over my shoulder in my left ear. "There are things you must do for me."

"I paid my money." I walked a little faster. Surely since I had shoes on, I could walk faster. "I owe you nothing."

A wad of spit came flying over my shoulder and landed on the ground in front of me.

"Thief! This woman is a thief!" The gypsy danced around me with her arms extended out in front of her, not letting me pass. "She stole my veil!" she seethed. "She's the intruder you seek!"

"What are you doing?" I hissed at her.

Her eyes were dark, squinted with malice set deep in them. She grabbed my wrist and spit again, this time landing on my shoe. A crowd had gathered around.

"You are just foul people." I pushed her aside.

She fell to the ground like I really did forcibly push her. She lay on the dirt ground. Her arm shot in the air, her finger pointed at me. "You are a thief!"

The crowd got rowdy. Their circle moved closer and closer to me as they stepped forward. Each of them gnashing their teeth, spitting, and yelling expletives at me.

Nervously I rubbed my hand around my wrist. My bracelet was gone.

"My bracelet." Frantically I looked around my feet, trying to ignore the angry mob.

"Mine now, *witch*!" The gypsy dangled my bracelet with her long fingers before she slipped it into the depths of her cloak. "Get her!"

Before I could run, a couple of men grabbed me. Another man threw me over his shoulder and started to march. I held onto my bag and tried to squirm my way off and out of his muscular grip, but I was going nowhere.

"Let me go!" I screamed moving side to side in hopes he'd drop me.

"Kill the witch!" the crowd screamed with their fists pumping the air.

"I'm not a witch!" I yelled back in hopes to save my life. "Mr. Prince Charming!" I screamed trying to lift my head to see if he was anywhere around.

It would come in awfully handy if he would live up to his duty of fairy-god cat.

The man turned around and walked backward. The crowd roared like he was slaying the big bad witch. I looked up.

The scary castle was getting closer. At that moment I knew I was about to get a tour.

Chapter Twenty Three

We didn't make it all the way up the hill before a horse-drawn wagon pulled up behind us. The man dropped me from his shoulder and on my butt into the wagon.

"Ouch!" I rubbed my leg where it had hit the edge and noticed Mr. Prince Charming crouched in the tall, thick grass on the side of the gravel road. Seeing him gave me a little more confidence. "Where are you taking me?"

"Silence thief!" The man clicked the reins and the horse bolted off, sending me flying backward.

"I'm not a thief. The gypsy took my twenty-dollar bill in exchange for the cloak and veil." I simply stated the facts because I knew this was all a misunderstanding. "She is the thief. She is a thief who took my bracelet."

"Silence thief!" he screamed in his gruff ogre voice. "You will be heard in court."

"Court?" My mouth dropped. "When is court?"

"It could be a couple of years or ten years. Depends."

"Years?" My throat tightened. I didn't have years.

Images of Oscar pushing a baby carriage with Arabella on his arm strolling through Whispering Falls danced in my head.

"I don't have years. Let me go!" I demanded to deaf ears and stomped my feet.

I grabbed the sides of the wagon and held on for dear life when the horse took off straight up to the castle.

"Stick her in the dungeon," the man driving the wagon told the guard who came out to get me.

My eyes drew up and down. He didn't look so tough in his little ballooning pants, bare feet, and blowsy top that looked like someone had ripped the sleeves off of it. His greasy scruffy brown hair could stand to use a good shampoo. The patches of hair on his face proved he was only a young boy who was trying to fit in with the others. Even his eyes were more innocent.

"Or you could just let me go." I smiled through the pain when he grabbed me shooting down my little theory that I could take him down.

He flung me over his shoulder. What was it with flinging me? I made sure to watch and make mental notes on where he was taking me. I was going to get out of this place somehow.

Before the heavy wooden doors closed behind us, Mr. Prince Charming darted in unnoticed. The halls were lit with candle sconces every few feet along the walls. The walls were draped with heavy tapestries.

"Is this really going to take years?" I asked the young man as he tossed me to his other shoulder.

He let out an audible groan when I landed.

"You can put me down. I can walk," I told him.

He stopped, bent his knees and leaned forward setting me on my knees. I stood there without moving in fear he would grab me up again.

"Oh," he sighed and put his hands on the small of his back stretching his torso back. He flung his hands above his head and then plunged down to the ground. He said, "I'm not cut out to carry women like that."

"Thank you!" I put my hands out in front of me and moved a little half-circle around him.

"Whoa." He put his arm out in front of me to stop me from going any further. "I put you down, not set you free. You have a crime to answer for."

I winced when he grabbed me by the arm and thrust me forward.

"Walk," he ordered.

I did what he told me to do.

"Tell me about this place." I was trying to make small talk to make a personal connection with him which was something I saw in the movies. If he recognized I was human, he might feel bad and let me go.

"It's almost as old as our village. We use the dungeon to hold thieves like yourself." He kept his voice low and mysterious. "It is rumored to have several secret passageways, but I have yet to find any."

"So this is your job?" I asked, this time out of curiosity.

"Yes."

"I own a homeopathic cure shop in Whispering Falls." It was good hearing Whispering Falls come out of my mouth. It made my situation seem a little less bleak.

"Whispering Falls. Hmmm…," he hesitated, "is that the village where everyone is welcome?"

"Yes. As a matter of fact that was the first rule I made when I became the Village President." I stopped when he grabbed me by the shoulder and pulled on a heavy metal round handle attached to a large wooden door. There was a winding staircase going down. He gestured for me to go. "I think everyone should be able to get along."

"You are the President of Whispering Falls?" His boastful laughter echoed, bouncing off the old stone walls. "And you are in Azarcabam stealing an old cloak with a fake jeweled veil?"

"I didn't steal it. I needed it to move around the village in order to find my missing friend." The future was starting to look bleak to me. Luckily Aunt Helena knew where I was and surely she wouldn't leave me here for years.

"Whispering Falls, huh?" he asked again. His heavy footsteps thundered down each step behind me.

"Yep." I let out a heavy sigh. The movies and TV shows made it look so much easier.

"Do you know Arabella Paxton?" he asked.

"You know Arabella?" In shock, I stopped dead in my tracks. He fell into me. I didn't even realize we were at the bottom when the door swung open and knocked me in the head, knocking me out cold.

Chapter Twenty Four

"Oh," I groaned. I didn't know what hurt worse, the large goose egg of a knot on my forehead or my back where they had laid me on the hard cold stone floor in one of the dungeon cells.

"How do you think I feel?" The male voice asked from across the cell. I couldn't see him through the dark.

I sat up and rubbed my head.

"What made you pass out this time?" he joked.

This time? I felt my torso. The guard wasn't too smart. They had left my bag strapped around my body. I reached in and grabbed my phone. I knew there was no way I would have coverage, but I did have the flashlight.

The man was crumpled up in the corner with his back to me.

"What do you mean 'this time'?" I asked him.

He rolled over. I dropped the phone from the shock when I saw it was Gerald.

I scurried over to him, grabbing the phone on my way over.

"Gerald," I gasped. "I'm so glad to see you."

"Don't get too excited. Both of us are in here." There was doom and gloom in his voice, but I could see some relief in his eyes. Plus he melted when I grabbed him, sucking him into a big bear hug.

"At least we are together." I didn't want to let go. "And Mr. Prince Charming is around here somewhere."

Both of us knew that we had a little shot of getting out with my ornery cat sneaking around.

I pulled away and put the phone light between us. It illuminated just enough for us to see each other's face. There was a little more hope then what I had seen before in his eyes.

"We have to find a way to get out of here." I moved the light source around the dungeon looking for any type of opening or crack.

I racked my fingers along the large cement block. Light debris fell to the floor in little crumbles.

"Ugh!" I screamed. Frustrated, I beat my fist on the cold and damp wall. "Why aren't you helping me?" I wailed through a veil of tears that had formed on my lids. "Don't you want to get out of here?" I pleaded and cursed under my breath.

"There is no reason to live with my sweet dear Petunia dead." His voice was tight as he spoke. He let out a whimper before his body deflated back down to the floor.

"Petunia isn't dead," I assured him. "Not awake, but not dead."

"You mean she survived the spiders?"

"How did you know about the spiders?" Incomplete thoughts swirled in my head.

Did he put the spiders there? Did Arabella? Eloise did say that anyone who had access to flowers and herbs had access to the Vermillian Spiders. Did the gypsy have anything to do with Arabella? How did Gerald tie into all of this? What about his relationship with Arabella? *Tramp.*

Never in a million years did I ever see my life turning out to be a spiritualist. And I wasn't going to die in some dungeon. Right about now, I really wished I was back at the Locust Grove flea market selling my little potions I had made in the shed.

"No the spiders didn't kill her." I didn't know if I should tell him about my going to see her, but we were stuck in here and there was no real reason not to. Our situation wasn't looking so great. "I went to the hospital to see her. I noticed you didn't."

He hung his head in shame.

"I had broken into Glorybee and got some evidence that one of my customers had left in her shop." I looked at him with a critical eye.

"This customer," his voice was softly low. A little too softly, as if it was a sign of danger and he knew it was a sign of danger. "Did she have short hair, emerald earrings?"

I nodded. I had a niggling suspicion that he was holding something back.

"Did she ask you for a potion?" He got into the crawl position, looking me dead in the eyes.

I nodded.

"Oh God June!" he cried out and stood up on his knees with his hands in his head.

His reaction pulled a sick feeling out of me. There was not an ounce of hope he was giving me.

Stay strong, my intuition told me.

"What Gerald?" Swaying a bit, I leaned up against the wall. *Please don't faint*, I begged myself. This was definitely not the time.

"Please, tell me," I said hoarsely and reached my hand out to touch Gerald's, "why you are in here?"

"There is something you need to know," his voice trembled. "I'm from Azarcabam and I have committed a crime that has not only affected my life but has left my precious Petunia hanging on for dear life."

"Are you saying you are the one who hurt Petunia?" I didn't care where he was from. All I cared about was clearing my name in order to get home to claim Oscar. I had no idea how much time had gone by since I had left Whispering Falls. The limited daylight and lack of schedule had thrown me off.

"Not directly." He drew back. "My past does."

"What happened?" I didn't want to let him know the gypsy and Madame Torres had told me his past was what I needed to figure out in order to clear my name of this mess and how I found the spiders and the Thickeris Plant at the gypsy's place.

"Wait," he stopped. "Why are you here?"

"I came looking for you." There was no reason to be blunt. Especially since I was going to have him arrested for the crime. "You suddenly skipped town. Arabella Paxton convinced Sheriff Lance that I was the one who hurt Petunia."

"No, no." He shook his head, visibly shaken. "No."

"Yes," I said firmly. I wasn't going to let little Miss Pretty Flower get her cute way. "Yes. She wants Oscar for herself. I saw her talking all secretive to you." I pointed at him. "And she sent Petunia flowers from me. Orchids of all things. And she sent me flowers with Thickeris Plant which was used in a potion I made for a client's barren daughter. Don't tell me she doesn't have it out for me."

I crossed my arms. Thinking about her made my blood boil and want to desperately get out of here faster.

I felt my hand around the old rock wall to find one of those secret passageways the young guard had heard about.

"How do you know the customer?" I asked. He hadn't finished telling me about her.

"Ezmeralda is my wife," Gerald's voice was muffled.

"What did you say?" I turned back around. "It sounded like you said she *is* your wife." I laughed at the trick my ears were playing on me. "Sorry, I'm sure it's from being taken prisoner in a foreign village." I put my finger in my ear and wiggled it back and forth to get my hearing back.

"You heard right. I'm married and we are from here. We are both Dark-Siders. I never told anyone. When I moved to Whispering Falls years ago, I fudged my records." There was no pride in his voice.

"Oh my God." I held my hand up to my mouth. Suddenly I felt like I was going to throw up. "Does Petunia know?"

"No." Gerald's head hung down.

"Does *anyone* in Whispering Falls know?" I asked. I know he had said no one knew, but maybe he had told Izzy or someone and they would know we were here.

My knees felt weak. My stomach hurt. I slid down the wall. Mr. Prince Charming crept through the small bars of the dungeon and rushed to my side.

"No. Only Mary Lynn and Arabella. Arabella wouldn't hurt a fly."

"How do you know that?"

"Because I wouldn't." Arabella grabbed the bars on the other side, the free side of the dungeon.

Meow. Mr. Prince Charming did figure eights around Arabella's ankles letting me know she was a safe person. *Purr, purr.* He did an extra little rub-up to assure my cautious soul.

"Hi Dad." Arabella smiled. Her eyes softened. Gerald stood up and rushed over to the bars, taking Arabella's hands into his, kissing them.

"Dad?" The anger welled in my voice. I snapped my fingers in the air. "Gerald." I held a steady and stern voice. "Your daughter?" I pointed my finger in the air. My mouth rambled like the train I had ridden in on. "Who is her mother? Does Petunia know she is your daughter?"

Daughter? Things were becoming very clear.

"So your daughter moves to Whispering Falls and opens a shop. Your *wife* finds out, from her," I jabbed my finger her way, practically blaming her for what happened, "and she and your wife wreck havoc on our sweet town all because you couldn't keep it in your pants?" I screamed.

Mr. Prince Charming circled the perimeter of the ten-by-ten old stone cell. Every few steps he would touch a stone as though he was looking for something.

"Stop it!" I yelled at Mr. Prince Charming. He was making me nervous and I was on edge.

"I'm not sure how it all happened. I hadn't planned on getting married again. Ezmeralda is a crazy gypsy." Gerald wasn't lying. She was two kinds of crazy—scorned wife crazy and gypsy crazy.

"June, I had to have a fresh start. My grandmother told me about Whispering Falls." Arabella showed some signs of regret, which was a little more endearing. "I don't want to live the life of a gypsy and when I told my mom, she wouldn't hear of it. That is when Grandmother and Dad helped me escape, only Mom had all her little friends watching us and we didn't know it."

"And Oscar?"

"Oh," she shook her head, "he was only to distract you from what was going on. I knew Mom was lurking around. She told me that if I got your goat and picked out that ring you wanted that she would give Dad the divorce and no one would ever know. Only you were too smart for her."

"Let me clear this up." I sucked in a big deep breath of air. "You aren't after my man?"

"No, he's all yours if I can get you out of here." Suddenly I was liking Arabella a little bit more.

Rowl, rowl. Mr. Prince Charming batted at an old stone. He rubbed his body to the right, turning and then rubbing his body to the left, pawing it in between. *Rowl!* He screeched wanting our attention.

"Your bag and your cat are going nuts." Gerald pointed out that Madame Torres was glowing a bright fiery red.

"Oh." I pulled her out and sat her between me and Gerald.

She showed us Main Street in Whispering Falls. The geraniums that hung in the baskets were lifeless, the dark sky was grey, the streets were empty.

Gerald groaned.

I looked in horror. It wasn't the same city I had left. Petunia was right. Everything in Whispering Falls was dying.

Madame Torres scanned the stores and zeroed in on Magical Moments. The beautiful flower bodice was no longer vibrant with colors. It was brown and the flowers had fallen on the ground in a puddle.

"No! I didn't do it!" Oscar was being cuffed on the inside of the shop by Colton. "I would never hurt anyone!" he screamed. "I'm putting in a security system for Arabella."

Mary Lynn was behind him. Her small balled-up cheeks were stained from the tears dripping out of her eyes. She stood in silence as they took Oscar away. To me that was a sure sign she knew who was behind this whole mess.

A couple of spiders scurried across the floor. There were spider eggs all over the floor, breaking open faster than Colton could step on them. The color creations in Magical Moments were dying by the second. Closely I watched spiders barely touch a leaf, instantly killing the flower.

"I'm telling you! Find June Heal! Find Arabella. She is the one who hired me!" he shouted, jerking his body to the left and right.

"You have to break a few eggs to make an omelet," I gasped recalling Faith Mortimer's Whispering Falls Gazette headline. "What?" Gerald shook his head and eyed me like I was crazy. "Ezmeralda is behind those Vermillian Spiders!" Gerald voice was loud and boisterous. "The headlines. Faith told us about the eggs. She was warning us about the spiders."

Mr. Prince Charming continued to bat at the stone.

"Stop that crazy cat of yours!" Gerald demanded.

Madame Torres lit up again, grabbing our attention.

"Oscar Park, you are hereby under arrest for the—" Colton threw Oscar in the Whispering Falls jail cell and slammed the door shut.

"What?" I grabbed the glass ball and shook it. "What did he say?"

Madame Torres went black.

Chapter Twenty Five

I slumped back down. Defeated. Angry. Sad. Bitter. All the emotions twirled around my insides knowing there was nothing I could do.

"June?" Gerald's voice was a little less rigid and more tender. "June?"

Slowly I lifted my head.

"Arabella help us," Gerald told her.

"I snuck in here. If Mom or her minions find me, I will be right with you in there." She crawled around on the ground searching for anything to open the cell doors to let us out.

He rubbed his mustache before reaching over in the darkness to grab his top hat. His hand ran along the rim knocking off the dirt and placed it back on his head. "We are Dark-Siders. I have always lied to Isadora Solstice. But you, when you came, you gave light to my world. There is nothing but darkness and sadness here. My Arabella is talented." His eyes caught mine. They bore deep to my soul, stirring my intuition. "She is a medium. She can talk to the spirits who have left this world."

"You mean…" I held back tears forming in my eyes. "You mean she can see Darla? You can see my mom?" I asked with an urgent voice.

Without saying a word, she nodded.

Mewl. Mr. Prince Charming hadn't stopped pawing at the stone.

"Only an Ancient Goth could bring Vermillian Spiders out of Azarcabam." Gerald was putting two-and-two together. "Which means that Ezmeralda not only used her wicked powers but she used her own daughter to bring harm to all of Whispering Falls."

"Ancient Goth?" There were so many new things I was learning about the spiritual world. Why on earth did Isadora Solstice appoint me as the Village President when I clearly knew nothing about the spiritual world?

"I'm afraid it is a wedding gift from my wife, Ezmeralda." Gerald hung his head, defeated, broken.

"And she was punishing you by hurting Petunia?" I asked and crawled over to where Mr. Prince Charming continued to pace back and forth.

"Yes," he whispered. "I have been trying to get the divorce from the Ancient Council and with Mary Lynn's help."

"Does Petunia know any of this?" I asked and ran my fingers along the edges of the stones. Mr. Prince Charming sat, a proud look on his face.

"No."

"Is that why you wanted to wait to have the wedding?"

"Yes." His one-word answers were making everything *so* clear. "She doesn't know about Arabella either."

"Oh." My finger must've triggered a secret passageway. The stones fell to the ground in crumbles, exposing a light tunnel.

"Got it!" Arabella held a key up in the air. She quickly unlocked the cell door. She pointed to the secret passageway. "We have to go that way though. The front of the castle is filled with guards and cheering crowds."

"Cheering crowds?" I asked.

"They love a good hanging here." She held her hands in the air doing a gesture of a hanging. "You, my dear, are next in line," she warned as her eyebrows cocked.

Gerald jumped up behind me and grabbed Arabella in a big hug reminding me of the scene I had witnessed in the back of The Gathering Grove where they were hugging.

Now I knew why Arabella was telling him that he couldn't go through with the wedding.

All of us looked deep in the tunnel. The cobwebs were thick, which meant no one had been down there in a long time.

"Let's go!" I motioned for them to come on as I threw my bag over my shoulder. "Today is not a day I planned on dying. I have to get back and save Whispering Falls."

"And Oscar?" Arabella smiled.

"Especially Oscar." I smiled back in a peace-offering kind of way.

"Wait." There was caution in Gerald's voice. He put his hand out, motioning me to move out of the way. He stepped into the hole and took a closer look at the webs. "If these are Vermillian webs, we will not make it out alive."

I shivered. "No!" I yelled after Mr. Prince Charming who darted right on in.

"It appears to be fine. We can go." Gerald smiled for the first time since I had seen him.

Without another word, we followed my precious fairy-god cat through the underworld of Azarcabam. The tunnel ended right on the outskirts of town, exactly where I had started. There was the old locomotive waiting for us.

None of us looked back as we each stepped aboard the old rickety hunk of steel, taking a seat on the red velvet benches.

We held on to the sides as the train's wheels turned and creaked along the rails. The dangling tassels hit the passenger windows in a rhythmic back and forth motion. Mr. Prince Charming curled up and closed his eyes.

"Now what?" I asked Gerald, but was afraid of his answers.

"Well," he rubbed his hand down his face. "We have to find Ezmeralda. She holds the key to ending this."

"Exactly how do we do that?" I asked knowing good and well I wasn't going back to Azarcabam any time soon.

"The only way for Arabella to live in Whispering Falls would be to get the permission of the Ancient Council, which Ezmeralda sits on as the Ancient Goth. That has to be my number one goal." His lips thinned. Sadness stood on his face. "I will have to say goodbye to Petunia. Ezmeralda will never grant me a divorce, nor will she let Petunia live if I ask for one."

"How can we stop her? How can we get her to grant the divorce?" There had to be some way.

"There are ways. But we have to capture her, which is hard to do since she is a teletransporter." Gerald's words only confirmed my worst nightmare; Ezmeralda was not going to go down without a fight.

"I'm sorry I accused you of doing all of these things." I felt like I needed to clear the air before the train dropped us off.

"I'm sorry too." Arabella reached out and squeezed my hand.

"Here is the ring." I opened my bag. The ring didn't seem so important any more.

"Ring?" Gerald was confused.

I reached in my bag and felt around for the vintage ring from Bella's Baubles I had found in Gerald's room back in Azarcabam.

Once I found it, I held it out in my palm.

"Where did you get Petunia's ring?" he asked.

"I found it on the floor of your room back in Azarcabam."

"Ezmeralda," he whispered. "She must have gone to see Petunia and took it off her finger. When Arabella told me to get the ring, I thought she saw Petunia looking at it.

She said Petunia wanted it. It's your ring?" He sounded more confused.

Something didn't add up. I didn't tell him that Arabella had seen me in Bella's and overheard me tell Bella that I wanted the ring. I decided to keep it to myself.

"No. Not my ring." I smiled.

The train came to an abrupt stop. We held onto the edges of the bench and swayed back and forth along with the tassels until it was safe to stand. The door flung open and the stairs descended.

Mr. Prince Charming ran out before Arabella, Gerald and I got our footing to stand.

"I guess we are home." Gerald walked over to the steps and looked out.

"Home." Arabella nodded. "That sounds and feels nice."

We were in the wheat field where it all started. The wheat swooshed with the night wind. In the distance, the sky was still dark and grey over Whispering Falls. The deadness filled the air.

"How do we breathe life back into the village?" It might seem like a silly question, but it was a necessary one.

"We have to get Ezmeralda to confess." Gerald declared like it was going to be easy as pie.

"How do we do that?"

"We wait." *Ahem*, he cleared his throat, buttoned up his coattails, and straightened his shoulders. With his head held high, he took the first step off the train with me and Arabella following closely behind.

Chapter Twenty Six

"Welcome to Whispering Falls, A Charming Village," read the old beat-up wooden sign that stood in the middle of the wheat field. I smiled. Reading those words sent a joy through me.

"Are you ready?" I looked back at them. He was again the vision of class as he stood in perfect posture. It was the only Gerald I knew before my little trip to Azarcabam. Arabella was as beautiful as ever.

Without a word between us, they nodded, not looking at me, but across the wheat field.

I touched the wooden sign. The field parted. The brick pathway appeared. We took our first steps, knowing the path would lead us straight to Whispering Falls.

There wasn't a word spoken between us as we got closer to the village. The grey clouds had darkened to an almost deep black. My cottage was eerily silent as we passed it.

Gerald announced. "I have to get to Colton and clear all of this up."

My intuition hit me. A deep-rooted fear sent a chill to the depths of my bones. What if Colton didn't believe us? What if we couldn't get Ezmeralda?

"How do we get Ezmeralda here?" I shuddered to hear his answer.

He stopped at the top of the hill, looking down on Whispering Falls. He turned to me and placed his hands on my shoulders. "She loves a good fight. She'll be here. June," he chose his words carefully, "when you came to Whispering Falls, we knew you were the one who could move the spiritual world forward. You were the chosen one. As a member of the village council, I encouraged them to vote you as the new President because I thought you would be able to bring the two spiritual worlds together."

Without asking questions, I knew he was talking about the Good-Siders and the Dark-Siders.

"You made the initial steps and closed some of the distance by making Whispering Falls a joint community." He smiled. "It was everything we had hoped for. But there are Dark-Siders who will never want that day to come. They are still looking for the Ultimate Spell that is held deep within the Good-Siders."

The Ultimate Spell. I groaned remembering how I had already had to battle one Dark-Sider over the spell that would bring the spiritual world to an end.

"You know as well as I know, if the ultimate Dark-Sider got their hands on the spell, it would be all over for us." Gerald was giving me a warning.

"Do you mean that Ezmeralda could be the ultimate Dark-Sider?" My mouth dropped. My gut told me the answer before he confirmed it.

"Yes." He dropped his hands. We both turned toward Whispering Falls, taking in what can happen if the wrong sorts of spiritualists come to the city.

"Do you think Ezmeralda is here?" I knew these questions stung him to his core, but they were questions I had to ask.

"I don't know." He held his arm out and pointed toward the village. "That is what you and I have to find out."

"I can get her here," Arabella chimed in. "I will go back and live my life as a gypsy if it means saving Whispering Falls from her."

"No!" Gerald gasped, breaking down into tears and grabbing his daughter.

"Let's just see how things go." I began the journey into the city like I had done every single morning over the past year. Plus I knew the police station like the back of my hand since I had spent so much time there with Oscar when he was the police chief.

A couple of fireflies darted around us, which clued me in that it was night time in Whispering Falls. The fireflies were the teenagers in the spiritual world who were taken from us at a much too early age. Their souls came back in the form of the fluttery little lighted creatures.

"Go on." I batted at them. I didn't want them to break our undercover. If Colton or anyone saw them, they would know the nosy teens were up to something.

The station was dark. I motioned for Gerald and Arabella to follow me. I looked around for Mr. Prince Charming, but I didn't see him. The carriage lights that lined Main Street were dimly lit, not the vibrant glow that used to light the way for our magical village.

There was a tiny basement window in the back of the police station where I used to sneak into Oscar's apartment when I would bring him a morning coffee or a good morning kiss. We always left it unlocked and since Colton lived with Ophelia above Ever After Books, I knew the only person in the jail was Oscar, leaving us full access to the apartment I was sure no one had touched since Oscar had left.

I was right. The window was still unlocked. I pushed it up and started to climb in. Once inside, I looked out at Gerald who was much larger than I.

"If you think I'm going to try to fit in that hole, you are crazier than I thought you were, June Heal." He took his top hat off, held it to his chest and drummed his fingers on it.

"Hold on." I held my finger up and let Arabella slip in behind me. "I can let you in the door."

I shut the window back, keeping it unlocked of course, and flipped on the light switch. The basement apartment was exactly how Oscar had left it. After all, when he denounced his spiritual heritage, the Order of Elders, including Mary Lynn, immediately stripped him of his gift.

Abruptly I stopped when I saw the picture Chandra had taken of Oscar and me on our first Hallow's Eve parade in Whispering Falls. I was looking straight at the camera with a big grin on my face. Oscar's arms were around me and he was kissing me on the cheek.

I touched my cheek with one hand and used the other to stroke the picture before I stuck it in my bag. It was a memory that couldn't be taken away from me, even though Oscar didn't remember it.

"That's so sweet." Arabella stood behind me.

"No more time to waste. He's up there waiting to be rescued." We made our way up the back steps that led to the office part of the jail, including the cell where Oscar had to be.

"June Heal, I've never been so glad to see you." Oscar gripped the bars on the cell door. "Get me out of here. I'm never coming back to this crazy town again. And this means I'm not doing your alarm system." He pointed at Arabella.

"Shh," she warned him. He glared at her.

I didn't say a word. I looked out the front windows to make sure there wasn't anyone outside who could see me.

"My mom was here. She knew you were coming. She waited." Arabella picked up a jar of Vermillian Spiders that was unopened. "She isn't going to let my dad marry Petunia and she isn't going to let Petunia live. And she is planning on killing the entire village."

"You've got that right." The voice came from the deep darkness of the air.

"Show yourself," I demanded.

The light switched on. I knew the woman standing before me.

"What the hell?" Oscar stumbled back in the cell with his mouth wide open.

"Nice to see you again, June Heal." She put her hand out for me to shake.

My eyes narrowed. Her power was so strong. There was nothing I could do to her. I was helpless.

"Do something June!" Oscar screamed.

"Like what? Kill her with my intuition?" I quipped.

"My daughter. My dear dear daughter. Yes, you helped me out more than you know." Her voice dripped, a smile crossed her face. "I came to your little shop, June, which is very charming. I had to see exactly who we could pin this little murder on since there was no way I was handing over my family to the likes of a tree hugger."

Her laughter, soaked with evil, filled the station.

"Since you seemed so jealous of my dear cheating husband and his filthy friend, it was a no brainer." She swept across the room in her cloak and veil. The black onyx jewels dangled around her face. There was an onyx ring placed on her ring finger. Much larger and prettier than the little vintage one from Bella's. "After all, you don't have anything to live for. Right dear?" She looked over at Arabella.

"I'm sorry June." Arabella hung her head. "I wanted so bad to tell you that your mother has been around you since she left and she wanted to give you a direct message."

"What is the message?" I ran over to her. I would do anything to hear from my mom.

"Don't say a word!" Ezmeralda ordered Arabella to shut up. "She has what we need. The Ultimate Spell. I'm going to end this love affair with Gerald and whatshername once and for all."

"Wait!" I pleaded. "I will give you whatever it is you want if you just tell me what my mom said."

The words came out of my mouth before I could stop them. She was right. I didn't have anything anymore. My parents were dead, Oscar didn't remember me and I couldn't save Whispering Falls from her.

"I'm freaking out in here." Oscar paced back and forth. If he didn't have feelings for me before now, he certainly wasn't going to ever.

"First you will hear our demands." Ezmeralda was pleased with my desperation. "You will give us your book of spells from A Charming Cure, the one Darla left you. Then you will denounce your spiritual gift and go back to the little frumpy shop you owned at the flea market in Locust Grove." She clasped her fingers in front of her. "That's all."

"Will Oscar remember me?"

"Remember you?" Oscar laughed out loud in a frightened sort of way. "I'm going to do my damnest to forget you!"

I shook my head. I couldn't focus on him at this moment.

"He will, but he will not ever be in love with you." The pleasure of her having the upper hand sparkled in her eyes.

"This is ridiculous June!" Oscar ran his hands through his hair.

"What will happen to Whispering Falls?" There was a reason she wanted the Magical Cures Book, but what? I had been over that book a million times. There was nothing special in it.

"That is none of your concern. You will not remember this dreary little place. You will go back to your life as you knew it." She swept across the room and stood next to me. She tilted my chin with her long finger. The black onyx ring shone bright in my eyes. "Isn't that right Arabella?"

I slid my eyes to see Arabella. She didn't say a word. She didn't even look up. She kept her face down to the ground.

"If I can't have either life, why would I do it?" Something wasn't making sense. "What is in it for me?"

"Simple." Her fingernail ran across my chin, cutting me like a knife. "You get to live."

"Ouch." I jerked back and put my hand up to my face. My blood was dripping from the cut.

"That?" She laughed. "That is nothing compared to what you will feel if you decide to go against me."

"Go against you?" I asked. Confusion danced inside me.

"June, I hate to break it to you, but you are the chosen one. The Good-Sider against the Dark-Sider." She flipped her cloak in the air. After the snap of the cloth, there appeared a hologram.

It showed an epic battle of two sides. I couldn't make out any faces, but I knew it was good verses evil, something I didn't want to be a part of.

"I will tell you that if you don't accept my generous offer, as the chosen one for the Dark-Siders I will have to end your life." She wrapped her hands around Arabella's arms. "Isn't that right Arabella?"

"June I'm so sorry." Arabella looked at me. There was remorse in her eyes.

"You see, it was all fun and games when Arabella decided to run away from Azarcabam. Then I found her here, with her father, who I had been trying to hunt down. I decided to disguise myself in each little shop before I found you. Instantly I knew you were the chosen one. I had been hunting you all my life." She walked over to me and then around me. "You are much younger than I thought and not all that wise, which really won't make killing you a lot of fun. But I will do what I will have to do if you don't accept my very generous offer. You see," she leaned in. We stood eye-to-eye, "My daughter has developed a serious fondness of you and I'd hate to kill you."

"So what are my options again?" They were already engrained in my brain, but I was trying to buy me some time for my intuition to kick in and tell me how to kick her ass.

"See," Ezmeralda looked over at Arabella, "I told you she was stupid. Why on earth would you want to come here and live?"

"Grandma Mary Lynn," Arabella started to talk.

"My mother is crazy!" Ezmeralda screamed.

"Hold it right there." The police door swung open. Colton had his wand drawn.

"Oh," Ezmeralda delighted in the fact he was there. "Let me see." She pointed her long finger between me and Arabella. "Which damsel in distress did you come to save? The little witch or my daughter?"

"I came to take you into custody for attempted murder of Petunia Shrubwood." Colton kept his eye on her, his gun pointed directly at her head.

"You mean to tell me she's *still* hanging on?" She turned and rolled her eyes. "I swear the Vermillian Spiders you get in stores nowadays are not nearly as potent as they used to be."

"Do you have any weapons for me?" Suddenly Oscar sounded a little more upbeat.

Colton threw him the cell keys and a wand at the same time, still keeping his wand on Ezmeralda.

"Dear young man, you need to walk back out that door before I must kill you." Ezmeralda delighted in toying with Colton. "And you." She threw her head back in bitter laughter. "You are just a little boy pretending to play wizard."

"Oscar, she's a Dark-Sider Spiritualist. Please do what she says or you will be killed. Guns or that wand will not hurt her," I warned him. "Well, not coming from you."

"Why June, you aren't as stupid as I thought." She swung her cloak around. Her eyelashes created a dark shadow down her face. "You might be fun to duel with in a battle for the Ultimate Spell." She scrunched her nose. "Like a little cat and mouse. Only I'm the big bad cat."

"Please Oscar," I begged. There was no way I was going to give up the love of my life. It was crystal clear what I was going to have to do. It was either me or her.

"Ezmeralda," Mary Lynn floated in the air. Her soft voice rang out, "my dear sweet daughter. Please go back to Azarcabam." Mary Lynn smacked the air, creating a fireworks display in the room, sending Oscar to the ground.

"Oscar?" I rushed over to his side.

"He's fine," Ezmeralda rolled her eyes. "It's my dear old crazy mom's way of making him pass out so he won't remember me killing you."

"You crazy sonofa..." I flung myself across the room. I didn't know how I was going to do it, but I was going to kill her one way or another.

My hands found their way around her neck and I squeezed as hard as I could. She flashed her onyx ring at me, knocking me across the room, sending me up against the glass window, shattering it to pieces.

"June! Let me handle it!" Colton screamed for me to stop.

Faintly I could hear Arabella in the background screaming for Mary Lynn to do something.

I opened my eyes.

Ezmeralda shouted out in pain. The onyx ring went flying in the air, landing next to my feet.

"Grab the ring!" Oscar shouted.

Without looking at him, I scrambled to my knees and grabbed the ring.

"You crazy old lady!" Ezmeralda shouted. She pointed at Oscar.

I looked over. He stood like the confident spiritualist police officer who had stolen my heart. His wand pointed at Ezmeralda. Colton was backing him up.

"You gave him his powers back!" Ezmeralda wrapped her cloak around her. A tornado of black smoke lifted her off the ground, sending her into thin air. A piece of paper floated from the sky.

"Oscar? Is it true?" I looked between him and Mary Lynn.

"He didn't deserve his punishment for trying to save you. The Order of Elders had been discussing giving him powers back. Since he was here to save us, when he isn't even a spiritualist, makes me believe he deserves his heritage."

"Oscar?" Cautiously I glanced at him.

He smiled, held the wand up to his lips and blew on the tip before putting it back in his holster.

"I still don't know how to use this thing." He patted the wand that was securely strapped on his hip. "Thank God I'm good at pretending."

I ran over and threw my arms around his neck. My heart soared when I felt his arms wrap around my body, squeezing it.

"What is going on here?" Gerald stood at the broken window.

Behind him, the sun was peeking out, sending the dark grey clouds far away from Whispering Falls. The dead brown geraniums that hung on the carriage lights sprung back to life.

"Good news!" Aunt Helena rushed into the police station. "Petunia is awake. She's going to be all right."

Gerald rushed over to Arabella. She bent down and grabbed the paper, giving it to Gerald.

"She signed it Daddy." Arabella burst into tears.

"She signed the divorce papers. She gave Arabella permission to live here." Gerald held the paper close to his heart.

Mr. Prince Charming darted in and dropped my charm bracelet at my feet. Oscar picked it up and clasped it on my wrist.

A round of cheers could be heard all over Whispering Falls. Everyone had gathered outside on Main Street as the Karima sisters zipped through town in their ambulance, stopping at Glorybee Pet Shop.

Constance jumped out before Patience and opened the back door. The sisters helped Petunia out from the back.

She looked happy, refreshed. Her hair was back up in the normal healthy bird's nest.

"Hello!" She waved to the citizens. Birds from all over flew in her hair, one-by-one taking their rightful place.

Gerald and Arabella rushed to her side.

"I love you." Petunia flung her arms around Gerald and Arabella. "I love you both."

Happily they marched into Glorybee together. The animals from inside the pet store shrilled with delighted. "What about Ezmeralda?" I asked. "It seems she and I have some unfinished business to take care of." I gulped knowing what was written in the spiritual stars. "She's gone. She won't be back for a while." Oscar took the ring from me and gave it to Mary Lynn. "Without the power of the ring, she will have to figure out how to get the Ultimate Spell. Which will be virtually impossible."

"Just to clarify." I stepped back and looked at Oscar, Mary Lynn, and Colton. "Oscar has his spiritual powers back?"

"What are you talking about?" he asked.

Mary Lynn and Colton gave me the silent *shh*, telling me that Oscar didn't remember not having his powers.

"And I have the Ultimate Spell buried in my potion book from Darla?"

They all nodded.

"How do Oscar and Colton know each other?"

"June, don't you remember?" Aunt Helena asked. "They met at sorcery school at Hidden Halls, A Spiritualist University." She smiled. "And they are co-sheriffs of Whispering Falls." She winked. It was like the time had passed and Oscar didn't know he had denounced his power.

"Oscar, I think you need to take your girlfriend home to rest." Colton laughed. "That bump on the head from hitting the glass window might have given her a little concussion."

"Girlfriend?" My heart filled with a warmth I hadn't felt in a long time.

"A...yea." Oscar wrapped his arm around me before pulling me closer. "I'm so glad she didn't hurt you. I would never let that happen." His vow was sealed with a kiss.

Chapter Twenty Seven

"I'll be with you in a second." The bell over A Charming Cure's front door rang when someone walked through it.

I was busy trying to make up a few potions to replace all the ones that had sold while I was away at Azarcabam. Faith Mortimer had done a great job taking over and had nearly sold everything in the shop.

In fact, I had offered her a full-time job since she was so good at selling, which she gladly accepted.

"It's just me. Take your time," Petunia said.

"Petunia!" I bolted around the partition. "What are you doing here?" I looked up at the clock. "You only have a couple of hours before the wedding."

"I wanted to stop by and thank you." Joy bubbled in her eyes. "If it weren't for you, Gerald and I would have never been able to get married today."

"How are you?" I asked. "I know it had to be difficult finding out about him having a daughter and wife."

"Arabella is a sweetheart and you know how crazy his ex is." She smiled.

We both knew how crazy his ex was without further discussing it. Deep in my soul I knew I was going to have see her again, but if it wasn't for another thirty years, that would be fine with me.

"Instant family." She laughed. She reached over and hugged me. A white dove popped its head out of her hair. I jerked away. "What? You didn't think I'd have my hair done for my wedding without doves did you?" She winked.

"I'm glad you are here." I moved around the counter and picked up the Village President Rule book. I held it close to my chest and walked back over to Petunia. "I want to give you your wedding gift."

I held the book out in front of me.

"What?" She looked confused.

"I'm stepping down as the Village President and giving it to you." I pushed the book toward her. "It's no secret that you wanted the job way more than I did. Plus you know Whispering Falls like the back of your hand."

She took the book. I noticed she wore a different ring than the vintage one Gerald had initially picked out for her. My ring.

"You know this doesn't get you out of being the chosen one, right?" she asked.

"I know." I forced a smile on my face. "This way, when the day does come and I have to face Ezmeralda, I'll be ready."

"June, are you sure?" she asked. Excitement escalated in her voice.

"I'm positive." My intuition told me it was the right thing to do and it hadn't failed me yet. "Hey, new ring?" I questioned.

"Yes. June, Arabella told us that Ezmeralda made her find out what ring you really wanted so it would fit into her plan of me dying. Of course when Arabella told Gerald I had picked it out, he went and got it." She patted my hand. "You and I both know it was your ring from the get-go. Gerald told me about the dungeon and how you had found the ring in the room."

"Oh, he told you all about Azarcabam?" I didn't know if he would tell her everything.

"Yes. And if you ever want to talk, let me know." She smiled. "I know you can't discuss it with Oscar because he doesn't remember everything like we do."

"I'm hoping to forget about it too," I confirmed. There wasn't anything I wanted more than to forget Oscar losing his powers.

"I guess I better get going. See you in a couple of hours." She held the book close to her body and walked out of A Charming Cure.

Within the hour, I had replenished all the regular potions that had been sold and cleaned up the shop. A Charming Cure would be open for business tomorrow, first thing in the morning since my last order as Village President was shutting the city down for the celebration of Gerald and Petunia's wedding.

"Honey, are you ready?" Oscar walked in. His blue eyes twinkled against his black tuxedo. His bright smile sparkled against his olive skin and Chandra had cut his coal-black hair perfect for the occasion. Mr. Prince Charming stood next to Oscar. He had a little black bowtie tied around his neck. It wasn't a secret that he loved Petunia and her shop.

"Almost." I held my finger up and slipped into the back of the shop. I had gotten here early to make the potions and I knew it would take up most of the day. I had brought my bridesmaid's dress with me. I yelled out into the shop, "Did you sleep okay?"

I slipped the orange dress on and glanced in the mirror. My charm bracelet jingled as I straightened my black bob. I stared at my reflection. I smiled. Having Oscar back made me feel so full and happy. I felt my bracelet and glanced down, looking at every single charm Mr. Prince Charming had given me.

"Any night I sleep next to my best friend is a good night." Oscar snuck up behind me, wrapping his arms around my waist. He nuzzled his face into my neck. His lips sent the pit of my stomach into a wild swirl. He tilted his head up and looked at us in the mirror. "You sure are beautiful."

"You're silly." I pulled away and walked back into the shop.

On the counter there were some June's Gems from Wicked Good, a lit candle, and a bottle of champagne with two flutes. Arabella, Eloise holding Madame Torres, Bella and Mr. Prince Charming stood behind the counter with smiles on their faces.

"Wow! When did you do this?" I smiled. All of his little surprises told me I had made the right decisions in my life.

"While you were putting your dress on." He grabbed my hands and held them between us. "June," Oscar bent down on one knee. He looked up at me. "I have known you all of my life. And there is no one I would rather spend the rest of my life with." He pulled out the vintage ring from Bella's Baubles out of his pocket. "This was your mother's ring. Bella had been saving it for you, so when Gerald came to get it, Bella knew something was brewing."

Bella stepped forward. "It was written in your stars to have the ring. I knew it would come back so I let Gerald buy it."

"I knew it was your mother's ring," Arabella stepped up next to Bella. She had been transformed back into the beautiful girl that had first stepped foot in Whispering Falls. "Because your mother told me." A tear dripped down her face. "I'm a medium. I want you to know your mother is here today. Her spirit has come forward several times since I lived here, only my mother wouldn't let me tell you."

I swallowed hard. Oscar stood back up and put his hand on the small of my back. He knew I needed his support. I was shaking.

"She wants me to let you know that she is proud of you. She is always with you. You will do the right thing in the spiritual world when the time comes. You will also rise above any evil and defeat it." Arabella stepped back, letting me know my mom's reading was done.

Oscar took my hands again and got back down on one knee. "June Heal will you give me the honor of being my wife and making me the happiest man in the world?"

He stood up and slid my mother's ring on my finger. It was a perfect fit.

"Yes!" I screamed throwing my arms around him. He swept me up, weightless in his arms. His kiss was the smoldering heat that got my cauldron going.

I glanced over Oscar's shoulder. Everyone was smiling. Even Madame Torres. Everything seemed great and fine in Whispering Falls, but my gut told me it wasn't going to be the last we had heard or seen of Ezmeralda.

Next time…next time, I was going to be ready for her.

About The Author

International bestselling author Tonya Kappes spends her day lost in the world of her quirky characters that get into even quirkier situations.

When she isn't writing, she's busy being the princess, queen and jester of her domain which includes her BFF husband, her teenage guys, two dogs, and one lazy Kitty.

Tonya has an amazing STREET TEAM where she connects with her fans on a daily basis. If you are interested in becoming a Tonya Kappes Street Team member, be sure to message her on Facebook.

For more information, check out Tonya's website, Tonyakappes.com, Facebook, and Twitter

Praise for Tonya Kappes

"Tonya Kappes continues to carve her place in the cozy mystery scene with the witty and endearing *Ghostly Undertaking* set in a small town that is as fun as it is unforgettable."
New York Times bestseller Dianna Love

"Full of wit, humor and colorful characters, Tonya Kappes delivers a fun, fast-paced story that will leave you hooked!"
Bestselling Author, Jane Porter

"Fun, fresh, and flirty, Carpe Bead 'Em is the perfect read on a hot summer day. Tonya Kappes' voice shines in her debut novel." Author Heather Webber

"I loved how Tonya Kappes was able to bring her characters to life." Coffee Table Reviews

With laugh out loud scenes and can't put it down suspense A Charming Crime is the perfect read for summer you get a little bit of everything but romance. Forgetthehousework blog

"This book was fun, entertaining and good to the last page. Who knew reading auras could get Olivia in so much trouble? Sit back, smile and cozy up to Splitsville.com, where Olivia does the dumping for you. There's heap loads of humor, a dose of magical realism, sprinkles of romance, and mystery when someone ends up dead!" Author Lisa Lim

Also by Tonya Kappes

Women's Fiction
Carpe Bead 'em

Olivia Davis Paranormal Mystery Series
Splitsville.com
Color Me Love (novella)
Color Me A Crime

Magical Cures Mystery Series
A Charming Crime
A Charming Cure
A Charming Potion (novella)
A Charming Wish
A Charming Spell
A Charming Magic

Beyond The Grave Series
A Ghostly Undertaking

Grandberry Falls Series
The Ladybug Jinx
Happy New Life
A Superstitious Christmas (novella)
Never Tell Your Dreams

A Divorced Diva Beading Mystery Series
A Bead of Doubt Short Story
Strung Out To Die

Small Town Romance Short Story Series
A New Tradition
The Dare Me Date

Bluegrass Romance Series
Grooming Mr. Right

Non-Fiction
The Tricked-Out Toolbox~Promotional and Marketing Tools Every Writer Needs

CPSIA information can be obtained at www.ICGtesting.com
Printed in the USA
LVOW04s0319310315

432680LV00025B/493/P